**BOOKS BY
ALEXANDER MCCALL SMITH**

IN THE NO. 1 LADIES' DETECTIVE AGENCY SERIES

The No. 1 Ladies' Detective Agency
Tears of the Giraffe
Morality for Beautiful Girls
The Kalahari Typing School for Men
The Full Cupboard of Life
In the Company of Cheerful Ladies
Blue Shoes and Happiness
The Good Husband of Zebra Drive
The Miracle at Speedy Motors
Tea Time for the Traditionally Built
The Double Comfort Safari Club
The Saturday Big Tent Wedding Party
The Limpopo Academy of Private Detection
The Minor Adjustment Beauty Salon
The Handsome Man's De Luxe Café
The Woman Who Walked in Sunshine
Precious and Grace
The House of Unexpected Sisters
The Colors of All the Cattle
To the Land of Long Lost Friends
How to Raise an Elephant
The Joy and Light Bus Company
A Song of Comfortable Chairs
From a Far and Lovely Country
The Great Hippopotamus Hotel
In the Time of Five Pumpkins

OTHER SERIES

The 44 Scotland Street Series
The Corduroy Mansions Series
The Detective Varg Series
The Isabel Dalhousie Series
The Paul Stuart Series
The Perfect Passion Company Series
The Professor von Igelfeld Series

OTHER WORKS

The Girl Who Married a Lion and Other Tales from Africa
La's Orchestra Saves the World
Trains and Lovers
The Forever Girl
Emma: A Modern Retelling
Chance Developments
The Good Pilot Peter Woodhouse
Pianos and Flowers
Tiny Tales
In a Time of Distance and Other Poems
The Private Life of Spies and *The Exquisite Art of Getting Even*
The Winds from Further West

IN THE TIME OF FIVE PUMPKINS

IN THE TIME
OF FIVE PUMPKINS

ALEXANDER McCALL SMITH

Pantheon Books
New York

FIRST AMERICAN EDITION
PUBLISHED BY PANTHEON BOOKS 2025

Copyright © 2025 by Alexander McCall Smith

Penguin Random House values and supports copyright. Copyright fuels creativity, encourages diverse voices, promotes free speech, and creates a vibrant culture. Thank you for buying an authorized edition of this book and for complying with copyright laws by not reproducing, scanning, or distributing any part of it in any form without permission. You are supporting writers and allowing Penguin Random House to continue to publish books for every reader. Please note that no part of this book may be used or reproduced in any manner for the purpose of training artificial intelligence technologies or systems.

Published by Pantheon Books, a division of Penguin Random House LLC, 1745 Broadway, New York, NY 10019. Originally published in hardcover in Great Britain by Abacus, an imprint of Little, Brown Group, a Hachette UK Company, London, in 2025.

Pantheon Books and the colophon are registered trademarks of Penguin Random House LLC.

Library of Congress Cataloging-in-Publication Data
LCCN 2025942822 (hardcover)
ISBN 978-0-593-70178-2 (hardcover)
ISBN 978-0-593-70179-9 (ebook)

penguinrandomhouse.com | pantheonbooks.com

Printed in the United States of America
1st Printing

The authorized representative in the EU for product safety and compliance is Penguin Random House Ireland, Morrison Chambers, 32 Nassau Street, Dublin D02 YH68, Ireland, https://eu-contact.penguin.ie.

This book is for Jenna Emmons.

IN THE TIME OF FIVE PUMPKINS

CHAPTER ONE

TERMITE MAN

IT WAS A LONG TIME since Grace Makutsi had first been employed as secretary of the No. 1 Ladies' Detective Agency, a business once described in the local paper as "the answer to the problems of those who have problems." She had more or less appointed herself to that position when, all those years ago, Mma Ramotswe, the agency's only begetter, had announced its opening. Mma Ramotswe had not originally envisaged having a secretary—how was a small business to pay such a person?—but she had not had the heart to turn her away.

For Mma Makutsi had been insistent. "It is most important, Mma Ramotswe," she said, leaning forward to emphasise her point, "for a future-looking business to have a professional secretary." She paused before concluding, "Like me—for instance."

Mma Ramotswe was not sure whether her business would be future-looking: she entertained only modest ambitions for it, and the way Mma Makutsi was talking made her wonder whether this rather pushy secretary might not be better looking for a position with a diamond-mining company. They had grand offices, those people—quite unlike the single room of the No. 1 Ladies' Detective Agency, which made no statement, even if its view was worth a thousand words: the acacia trees, so popular with Cape doves; the Botswana sky; the winding, dusty paths through the bush . . .

"Well—" she began, but got no further before she was interrupted.

"If you do not have a secretary," Mma Makutsi warned, "people will have no confidence in you. A business without a secretary?" She shook her head. "That cannot be much good—that is what people will say, Mma—they will all say that."

"Well, Mma—"

"I am especially interested in filing. It is very important to have a good filing system."

Mma Ramotswe sighed. "Mma," she said, "there is not much money. This business is only starting. We have no clients yet, I'm afraid. We may never get any—who knows?" She knew she sounded defeatist, but more than one person had warned her that many new businesses failed to survive beyond a few months.

Mma Makutsi had hesitated, but only briefly. Then she said, "That does not matter, Mma. You can pay me when the fees start to come in."

Mma Ramotswe sighed again, and then, not really knowing why she did so, agreed. There could be no mistaking Mma Makutsi's motivation: somebody who was prepared to work on a speculative basis was bound to be a keen and conscientious employee. And so it was that Mma Makutsi, graduate *summa cum laude* of the Botswana Secretarial College—with ninety-seven per cent in the final examinations—embarked on her career with the No. 1 Ladies' Detective Agency. "It was the best thing I ever did in my life," she said, but then immediately qualified her statement. "The best thing after I decided to study at the Botswana Secretarial College, that is."

Mma Ramotswe nodded. "That was a very good move, Mma. A higher education stays with you for the rest of your days."

"You're right," agreed Mma Makutsi. She looked at Mma Ramotswe, a certain sympathy in her expression. "I'm sure you would have done very well yourself, Mma, if you had been given the opportunity."

Mma Ramotswe had left school in her mid-teens. She had done well at Mochudi High School, but there were fewer options in those days, and her formal education had ended then. She would have liked to have gone on to further study—it was one of the regrets of her life that she had not done so—but she had been given a good start by her father, the late Obed Ramotswe, who had patiently taught her so much about the world around her, as a good parent should do. He had taken her on long walks in the bush outside the village, or out at the cattle post, and had introduced her to the complexities of the natural world. He had taught her the Setswana names of the plants they came across—and their traditional use—knowledge that was fast fading in Gaborone and other towns. Words were dying, quietly and unlamented, through lack of use on the lips of younger people; it seemed, at times, that only the old remembered, and as they in due course became silent, whole lexicons of vocabulary were heard no more.

He had instructed her, too, in the ways of the San people, who could survive even in the harshest conditions of the Kalahari—priceless, ancient knowledge that he had acquired from a man of that origin whom he had known and who was a tracker with the Wildlife Department. All of that she learned, along with so much else about the country in which they lived—its sayings, its story, the habits of its people. He was proud of such things, and he had made her feel proud too. "We are fortunate," he said, "to be who we are—to have been born in this peaceful country, with all that has been given to us." And it was true: they had been given so much. God, as Obed Ramotswe had once said, was even-handed in his treatment of peoples, but even he could not help himself from particularly favouring Botswana.

She had never forgotten any of these lessons, and in remembering them she felt that she was keeping alive the memory of a man who stood for all that she admired in her country and its culture.

Now, as Mma Makutsi made this reference to the difference in their educational opportunities, Mma Ramotswe reminded herself of what she had learned from her father and of what she had picked up simply by being an engaged citizen. You could learn most things, she thought, by simply keeping your eyes open and *listening*. That's where most people fell down—they would not listen. We spend a lot of time shouting at one another, Mma Ramotswe once observed. If we spent a fraction of that shouting time on listening, we would do far better. There would be fewer wars, she thought—and fewer tears.

Her train of thought was interrupted by Mma Makutsi's continuing observations.

"I have been very happy working here in the No. 1 Ladies' Detective Agency," she said. "It has been my calling."

She had certainly been successful. Employees who leave it to their employers to promote them may have a long time to wait, but this was not the fate of Mma Makutsi. She had somehow managed to promote herself, first to the role of senior secretary, then, without discussing the matter with Mma Ramotswe, to assistant detective, associate detective, associate director, co-director and so on, to the position she had most recently chosen for herself—executive president for development. This was a novel description and had rather puzzled Mma Ramotswe.

"I see that you are signing executive president for development on letters now, Mma," she had said. "This is an unusual title, is it not, Mma Makutsi?"

Mma Makutsi shook her head. "It is not all that unusual, Mma. There are many companies who have people in such positions."

Mma Ramotswe considered this. "So that makes me a . . ."

"You could be executive president for operations, Mma," said Mma Makutsi. "You are the one who started the business. I would not want to claim to have been that person."

Mma Ramotswe had shrugged. It did not matter too much, she thought, what Mma Makutsi called herself. People paid very little attention to the titles that people gave themselves in the working world. What mattered was whether the work of the business was done to the satisfaction of the client, and there was no doubt but that Mma Makutsi was efficient and, what was more, effective. If she wanted to be called an executive president for development, then that was a harmless enough ambition. We all had our little vanities, and no harm was done if one indulged such things in others.

IT WAS A MONDAY NOW—a day that Mma Ramotswe rather liked. She knew that there were many who took a contrary view, but she relished the feeling of freshness that came with Monday morning. The whole week lay ahead, and from the very first days of the agency there had been no shortage of unusual clients walking through the door. That was the interesting thing about her profession, she thought. If you ran a dry-cleaning business or a hardware store, you knew from the beginning what clients would want when they came to your door: in the world of dry-cleaning, the clothes that needed attention might differ, but the basic need was always the same; as was the case with the hardware trade: one customer might need nails while another might be looking for a brush to sweep the kitchen, but they all wanted something for the house or the yard. Nobody went into a dry-cleaner's or a hardware store to unburden themselves of some long-concealed secret or a nagging fear. That, by contrast, was often the reason why they made their way to the No. 1 Ladies' Detective Agency's office on the Tlokweng Road, and there, of course, they would find the listening ear, and the solace, that troubled people so sorely need.

And that was exactly what brought Mr. Excellence Modise to the agency at ten o'clock that Monday, without an appointment. He knocked at the door and did not enter until Mma Makutsi called out from within. That was a good sign—and both Mma Makutsi and Mma Ramotswe noticed it. There were far too many people, Mma Makutsi had observed, who simply barged in. They might remember to knock, but many of them did not wait for an invitation, which, in her view, destroyed the point of knocking in the first place. Was the knock in such cases simply intended to warn people inside— to give them time to stop whatever they were doing, if what they were doing was something that they did not want others to see? It was best not to think too much about these matters, Mma Ramotswe believed.

The man who came in was of average height, middle-aged— perhaps fifty, thought Mma Ramotswe—and, apart from one thing, not somebody who would attract much attention if passed on the street. But there was that one thing that would have made him stand out, and that was his outfit. As he introduced himself, both Mma Makutsi and Mma Ramotswe found their eyes drawn to the two-tone shoes, the red shirt, and the small strip of yellow tie across his shirt front.

The traditional courtesies were exchanged and the visitor was invited to sit down. Then Mma Makutsi said, "You do not have an appointment, Rra?"

Mr. Excellence Modise shifted his weight uncomfortably in his seat. "No, I am sorry, Mma, but I have been very busy-busy." He paused. "If you want me to go, I can come back some other time . . ." He looked about him. He glanced at the electric kettle, which Mma Makutsi had just switched on; his eye moved on to the empty in-tray on Mma Ramotswe's desk. ". . . some other time, perhaps, when you are under less pressure."

Mma Makutsi was quick to reassure him. "That does not matter, Rra," she said. "I think we can squeeze you in."

Mr. Excellence Modise smiled. "So, I am not too fat," he said.

Mma Makutsi frowned. She glanced at Mma Ramotswe, who also seemed puzzled by this remark.

"You said that you can squeeze me in," explained Mr. Modise. "I said that means I can't be too fat—otherwise you would not be able to squeeze me in. That is what I said. It is a joke, you see."

Mma Makutsi managed a strained smile. "Ah, I see. Of course. That is very amusing."

"Perhaps you might care for a cup of tea, Mr. Modise," said Mma Ramotswe. "Mma Makutsi was just about to make tea. We always have a cup at about this time in the morning."

Mr. Modise nodded. "That is very good of you, Mma."

Mma Makutsi rose to attend to the kettle. "Do you take milk and sugar, Rra?" she asked.

Mr. Modise raised a finger, as might be done by one making an important point. "Yes, milk, please, Mma. Sugar—no. Real men don't take sugar."

Mma Makutsi stopped in her tracks, halfway to the kettle. "I beg your pardon, Rra?" she said.

"I said: real men don't take sugar," said Mr. Modise. "That was another joke, Mma."

Mma Makutsi continued on her way to the kettle. "My husband takes sugar," she said. "He has sugar in his tea and also in his coffee. My husband is very keen on sugar."

Mma Ramotswe picked up the note of irritation in Mma Makutsi's voice. It would have been difficult not to do so.

"I'm sure that Mr. Modise was not suggesting there is anything wrong with men who take sugar," she said.

Mr. Modise waved a hand. "Of course not, Mma. It was just a remark."

Mma Ramotswe decided to take control of the situation. On occasion, people got off on the wrong foot with Mma Makutsi, and it was often very difficult, not to say impossible, to retrieve the situation afterwards. "Perhaps you might tell us, Rra," she said, "what we can do for you."

Mr. Modise sat back in his chair. "*If* you can do anything for me, Mma."

Mma Ramotswe smiled indulgently. She did not like verbal sparring; she did not like people who tried to be smart, and this Mr. Excellence Modise—and why the two jokes, she wondered—this Mr. Modise was clearly trying to impress.

"We do our best by all our clients," she said evenly. "There are some whom we cannot help, of course—some people whose problems are just too difficult. Then there are some cases where we just cannot unearth what people want us to find out, no matter how hard we try. Then there are some people whom we cannot take on as clients because they are on the wrong side of the law. But for most people, we can do at least something."

Mr. Modise nodded. "I hope you don't think I'm on the wrong side of the law," he said. "I hope you don't think I'm some sort of *tsotsi*."

He used an expression from over the border, usually applied to a young gangster. Mma Makutsi raised an eyebrow: you could not be a middle-aged *tsotsi*, no matter how you dressed. Mma Ramotswe looked embarrassed. "I would never think that, Rra," she said. "So please, just tell me what we might be able to do for you."

Mma Makutsi had now made the tea, and she passed a cup to

Mr. Modise before going back to her desk. She avoided making eye contact with Mma Ramotswe.

"I am a very successful businessman," Mr. Modise began. "I am the owner of Special Pest Services. You may have seen my vans. We deal with all sorts of household pests—and some industrial ones too."

Mma Ramotswe took a sip of her tea. "I have seen them, Rra. They have a picture of a bug running away, carrying its suitcase."

Mr. Modise beamed with pleasure. "That was my idea, Mma," he said proudly. "I chose that picture myself. Many people like it very much. They think it is very funny."

Mma Makutsi stared into her teacup.

"I have four branches in the country," Mr. Modise went on. "One here in Gaborone, one in Selibi-Phikwe, one in Francistown, and one up in Maun. They are all very busy. There are pests everywhere, you see. Termites in particular. They have been trying to eat the whole country for a long time now."

"You are right about that, Rra," said Mma Ramotswe. "I have a wooden fence in my garden, and it was eaten badly. The timber had not been treated properly."

"Oh, there is a lot of that about," said Mr. Modise. "You get these people who claim to know all about timber preservation, but they don't know what they're doing. They are fools, these people—and the people who engage them to deal with their timber are fools too—for choosing people who don't know what they're doing."

This was too much for Mma Makutsi. "It is not their fault," she protested. "They could not have known that these people knew nothing about termites. How could they? When it comes to timber preservation, we are all in the dark, I think."

Mr. Modise made a dismissive gesture. "They should check up on people before they do business with them. That is very obvious, Mma."

Mma Makutsi bristled. "Did you check up on us?" she asked.

Mr. Modise looked away. Mma Makutsi waited, but it soon became clear that she was not going to get an answer.

"Please continue, Rra," said Mma Ramotswe. "You were telling us that you have a business. Is there some problem with the business? Is that what brings you here today."

Mr. Modise adjusted his thin yellow tie. "There are no problems with the business," he replied. "It is a personal matter."

As he said this, he looked over his shoulder at Mma Makutsi at her desk.

"It's a private-private, personal matter, Mma Ramotswe," he continued.

Mma Ramotswe assured him that the No. 1 Ladies' Detective Agency was very discreet. "We are strict observers of the rules of confidentiality," she said. "We hear many things in this office, but we speak about none of them."

She stopped to think. That was true, she decided: she and Mma Makutsi were careful about talking of client matters with others. There were only one or two people who might become party to the confidences of the office; obviously one could discuss issues with one's spouse, that was always implicit, she thought—although some disagreed—and was licensed by the whole institution of marriage. Mma Makutsi had once expressed the view that this was why Catholic priests were not allowed to marry—it was because if they had wives they might be expected to discuss with them the secrets imparted to them in the confessional box. Mma Ramotswe was not sure about that, and had once raised the matter with a senior member of the clergy at the Anglican Cathedral in Gaborone. He had laughed and said simply, "I very much doubt Mma Makutsi's theory." And then he had added, in case there might be any residual uncertainty, "In fact, she's talking the most dreadful nonsense—silly woman."

Mma Ramotswe had been privately shocked by this response. It was not fitting, she thought, for a clergyman to describe anybody as a *silly woman*. To begin with, it showed a certain attitude towards women that had long been impermissible. In the past, men might have imagined that they could be dismissive of women, that they might suggest with impunity that women were bad drivers (untrue) and that they had no head for business (equally untrue), but now such remarks like that would be roundly condemned—not only by women, who had become accustomed to defending themselves, but also by enlightened men—of whom there were now so many, including, of course, Mr. J.L.B. Matekoni. For a clergyman to identify himself as one of these unreformed men was, in her view, unfortunate, but perhaps not too surprising: clergymen were men after all, and no doubt had their faults too, even if these might not be quite as bad as those of other men.

And quite apart from the general unacceptability of such a remark, there was the issue of inappropriateness when applied to Mma Makutsi, of all people. Did this man know about Mma Makutsi's ninety-seven per cent? Clearly not, because nobody who got that sort of mark could possibly be described as a silly woman.

Mma Ramotswe was never confrontational. She was tolerant of people's failings—we are all weak in one way or another, she thought—some of us, perhaps, being extremely weak in some departments—but one should be tolerant of such failings in others. Most people, she thought, were doing their best, but some of them—the people she sometimes described as "the weaker brothers and sisters"—needed to be reminded from time to time as to where they were going wrong. And this, she thought, was probably one of those situations.

She frowned, and the clergyman shifted on his feet in a distinctly uncomfortable way. "Of course—" he began.

He might have been about to qualify his discourteous dismissal, but he did not get the chance.

"I do not think it is right," Mma Ramotswe interjected, "for a man of the cloth, Rra, to describe a lady as a *silly woman*. It is not a charitable thing to say—about anybody."

"Well—" he stuttered, but did not get any further.

"Particularly," continued Mma Ramotswe, raising a finger, "when the lady in question happens to be the most distinguished graduate of her year at the Botswana Secretarial College."

"No, well—"

"So, we shall say no more about it," concluded Mma Ramotswe, adding, "I am sorry to have had to speak to you in this fashion, Reverend. But it is sometimes necessary to point out to people that they are not in touch with modern ideas. It is very important to be in touch with modern ideas." She paused. "Not all, of course: there are some modern ideas that are . . ."

"Complete nonsense?" suggested the clergyman, and they both laughed. The tension had been defused, but Mma Ramotswe's point had been made—and understood.

She remembered that now, as she thought of the categories of people who might quite properly be party to client confidences. She might discuss a case with Mr. J.L.B. Matekoni, and Mma Makutsi might talk to Phuti—that was the spousal exemption. But it was also permissible, she thought, to have at least one outside confidante to whom one might talk. That person could even be regarded as a member of staff—and therefore entitled to hear what clients said—the justification being that discussing a problem with another often helped to solve it. The person Mma Ramotswe chose for this role was, of course, Mma Potokwane, with whom she had shared so many professional secrets over the years, and who, time and time again, had come up with helpful insights. Of course, it was possible that Mma Potokwane might talk to her own husband about the matters that Mma Ramotswe had raised, but she had not enquired about that.

She watched Mr. Modise as he weighed what she had just said to him about client confidentiality.

He glanced again at Mma Makutsi, who had noticed his first look, and now repaid it with a challenging stare. "What about your secretary?" He lowered his voice as he spoke, but of course Mma Makutsi heard it. Its effect on her was electric. She sat bolt upright, and her large round glasses flashed in the light from the window.

Mma Ramotswe struggled to undo the damage. "Mma Makutsi is not a secretary," she said. "She is . . . management."

She swallowed hard. She was charitable in her view of others, but it was difficult to feel anything but intense dislike for this man. "Senior management," she said, trying to remember what it was that Mma Makutsi was now president of.

Mr. Modise became conciliatory. "I did not mean to be rude, Mma."

"Well, please tell us what you want, Rra," said Mma Ramotswe. "And I assure you—I have heard everything, and there is nothing that can shock me."

Mr. Modise closed his eyes, and by this involuntary gesture, he told Mma Ramotswe something important. This man, she thought, is insecure. He may be the terror of the country's termites. He may be dressed like a con man. His speech may be littered with unfunny jokes and bombastic references, but he was, at heart, a little boy who was frightened of the dark. The fact that he closed his eyes told her that he was trying to pluck up his courage.

"It is my wife, Mma," he said at last.

They waited. On the ceiling, suspended upside down by the tiny suckers on its toes, a minute white gecko was motionless, waiting for a foolhardy fly.

Mma Ramotswe did not need to make an effort to sound sympathetic—she *was* sympathetic. She would not wish on anyone unhappiness in that most important of relationships. "I see, Rra. I'm sorry."

On the other side of the room, Mma Makutsi's glasses caught the light again. She was perhaps a bit less understanding.

"My wife does not like me," Mr. Modise went on.

They waited for him to say something more, but he did not. Mma Ramotswe noticed that he was looking down at his hands.

"I am sorry to hear that, Rra," she said. "Are you sure?"

He nodded. "I love my wife very much, Mma. I would do anything to make her love me. I would pay one hundred thousand pula for some *muti* if I thought that it would make her fall in love with me. I would do anything, Mma."

Mma Ramotswe shook her head. *Muti* was a potion that some people believed could change the way people thought about them. It was an old belief, not held by educated people—a belief that belonged to an earlier, unenlightened time. A belief in *muti* was superstitious nonsense. "*Muti* does not work, Rra," she said. "That would be a waste of one hundred thousand pula."

"Oh, I know that," said Mr. Modise. "I was just saying that to show you that I would do anything to get my wife to change her mind about me."

Mma Makutsi now joined in. "Excuse me, Rra," she said. "But if you have a marriage problem, should you not go to one of these people who give advice about these things? There are such people, I believe."

Mr. Modise turned to face Mma Makutsi. "Yes, Mma, there are

such people. They are the aunties, aren't they? They are these aunties who are always telling you this thing or that thing. If I go to see them, they will say that it's my fault, because the aunties are used to blaming men. No thank you, Mma. No thank you."

Mma Ramotswe held up a hand. She saw the danger. "Oh, Rra, I'm sure that was not what Mma Makutsi was talking about."

But it was too late for an emollient intervention—you did not talk to Mma Makutsi like that—not to the Mma Makutsi who was an executive president for development and who had, moreover, achieved the unequalled mark of ninety-seven per cent in the final examinations of the Botswana Secretarial College.

"These aunties," hissed Mma Makutsi, "are very wise ladies, Rra. They have seen a lot of life, I can tell you. They are not like men who parade around in fancy shoes and yellow ties. They know far more about what's what than men like that, I think." She paused. "That is just my opinion, of course, but perhaps I am no better than these aunties you're talking about, Rra."

Mma Ramotswe tried again. "I think we should not get involved in a big argument about aunties and so on. I think we should look at this calmly."

"I am being calm," protested Mr. Modise. "This other lady is the one who is doing all the shouting."

"I am not shouting," shouted Mma Makutsi.

Mma Ramotswe shot her a glance. Professionalism was at stake here. *Never lose your temper with a client*, wrote Clovis Andersen, author of *The Principles of Private Detection*. *Bite your tongue rather than argue with your client, who may be emotionally stressed. Rise above the urge to repay rudeness with rudeness.*

Mma Makutsi realised that she had gone too far. "I'm sorry, Rra," she said. "I should not have said that. I did not mean it."

Mr. Modise laughed. "Many people say that they do not mean

what they say," he observed. "But I find myself wondering why they bother to say anything if they are then going to say that they do not mean it." He turned to look towards Mma Makutsi again. "But don't worry, Mma, I do not mind what people say. I am not one of these people who bear grudges against other people who say things about them. Do not worry about that."

Mma Ramotswe seized the opportunity to guide the conversation into safer waters. "May I ask you, Rra," she said, "what you would like us to do? Please remember that we are a detective agency—we are not a counselling service for people with marriage problems."

"I know that, Mma," Mr. Modise assured her. "But I was hoping that you would find out why my wife is so . . . so cold-cold towards me." He looked away. "I am not just talking about the blanket, Mma. I am talking about everything. When I talk to her, she often hums a tune, as if she is thinking about a piece of music. That is not very pleasant, Mma."

I am not just talking about the blanket. Both Mma Ramotswe and Mma Makutsi knew what that meant: it was an expression used in Botswana to refer to private matters of the bedroom.

It seemed now that Mr. Modise was struggling to say something that he found difficult to express. His voice cracking, he went on, "I think she has a lover, you see. I think that she is seeing another man."

Mma Ramotswe sighed. The conversation was now in very familiar territory. One of the most common inquiries that private detective agencies were obliged to take on was precisely this: to find evidence of infidelity. *Unfaithfulness*, wrote Clovis Andersen, *is the bread and butter of our profession. Unfaithfulness, I am sorry to say, is everywhere.*

"Do you know who this lover might be?" asked Mma Makutsi, her pencil poised above her notepad.

Mr. Modise shook his head. "I do not know."

"But do you have any evidence?" Mma Ramotswe enquired.

Again, Mr. Modise shook his head. "I have no evidence. But that is probably because they are being very cunning. These people who have affairs are cunning-cunning in what they do. They do not like to be caught." He paused, and gave Mma Ramotswe a pleading look. "That is why I have come to you, Mma Ramotswe. I have come to you because people say to me that you are not only a very kind lady, who likes to help people, but you are also very good at finding out what is going on. They say that you know everything that is happening in this town—that is what they are all saying, Mma."

"You are very kind," said Mma Ramotswe. "And I shall try to help you, Rra, because I can tell that you are unhappy."

"I am very unhappy," said Mr. Modise. "Here I am, the number one man in the country for dealing with termites, and yet my heart is a stone within me. And that is because my wife loves another man. I do not know who he is, but I must find out so that I can chase him away."

CHAPTER TWO

A VERY POLITE BOY

ON THE WALL of Mma Potokwane's office at the Orphan Farm was a noticeboard. It had been there for as long as she had occupied the room, and it bore the drawing-pin marks of a succession of notes, charts, and newspaper clippings. Staff rotas—who should be doing what, for how long, and who should take over when the shift changed—occupied a large part of the board, but there were numerous reminders to herself as well: meetings about this and that; details of appointments with officials; government circulars about infectious diseases and vaccination programmes—the entire business of a large children's home was displayed on this board. A notice would go up, stay up for a few days, and then come down, to make room for the next reminder, the next official bulletin.

There was one item, though, that was displayed permanently, and to which the eye of any visitor was invariably drawn. This was a sheet of laminated paper, pinned prominently in the middle of the board, and on which, in large letters, was printed the message: *What do children need? They need one thing: unconditional love. If they have that, they have everything.*

Mma Potokwane had prepared this notice on the office printer, and had then taken it to a stationery shop for lamination. The words were her own, but she discovered that, with the passage of time, their inadequacy became increasingly apparent. What they said about children's need for love was true enough—few would dispute that—but there were other needs, and these she had added to the list, using a marker pen. So, the message was changed to read: *they need two things*, and, after *unconditional love* was added *healthy food, with not too many fried dishes*. At a later date, a further amendment was made, and *two things* became *three*, with the addition of *a lot of outdoor exercise*. In due course, after further thought on the subject, Mma Potokwane had felt it necessary to cross out *three* and substitute *four*. The fourth requirement was *a regular routine*.

The list had been viewed by Mma Ramotswe on her visits to Mma Potokwane. She had commented favourably on the list of necessities, although there were other requirements that she might have added, had her friend asked for her advice. She thought, for instance, that children needed to be taught, if at all possible, to love their country. They also needed to learn to help with household chores, to be careful of snakes when walking in the long grass, and . . . well, the list would soon become very long once one started to think about it. Yet as it grew longer, the list's impact seemed to diminish. *All one needs is love* is a proposition far more memorable than a list of twenty or thirty needs.

That Saturday, Mma Potokwane was particularly concerned with the third requirement: the need for plenty of outdoor exercise. To an extent, the children looked after that need themselves, as they were always running around, playing games that afforded them plenty of robust physical exercise. This was particularly the case with the young boys, who seemed incapable of walking and would launch themselves headlong at running pace whenever they needed to get anywhere—even a short distance. Alongside this natural expenditure of energy, there was plenty of organised activity, including enthusiastic games of football, in which more of the girls were now beginning to join.

But that Saturday was the annual sports day, when people from the local community flocked to watch the track events competed in by everyone: from the smallest children, the three- and four-year-olds, to the lanky seventeen-year-olds who were in their final few months in the home. The housefather, Mr. Kitso, ensured fair play and kept a list of the victors in each of the events. At the end of the afternoon, prizes would be awarded to winners—small trophies to mark the highest jump, the fastest one-hundred-metre sprint, the first past the post in the egg-and-spoon race.

Mma Potokwane had invited Mma Ramotswe to attend, and she had readily accepted the invitation. They stood together on the sidelines, Mma Potokwane wearing the wide-brimmed straw hat that she brought out for such occasions, and Mma Ramotswe sheltering from the sun under the large red umbrella that Mr. J.L.B. Matekoni had given her for her last birthday.

"The children seem very excited," remarked Mma Ramotswe. "There is so much noise, Mma. Listen to all the squealing."

Mma Potokwane smiled. "It's an odd thing, Mma," she said. "I am so used to it that I do not notice it at all. It is always there—like the sound that cicadas make in the bush. You know that sound? That *screech-screech*."

"I know it," said Mma Ramotswe.

"But I wouldn't want the children to be silent," Mma Potokwane went on. "That would be very strange. It is the one thing that worries me—if a child is silent. In my experience, that means that the child is sad. And as often as not, that will be because the child has had some dreadful experience."

Mma Ramotswe agreed. It saddened her to think about it, but distressing things still happened to children. So much progress had been made in looking after children, in outlawing child labour, in protecting children from the violence of powerful adults, but nothing you did would ever be enough to banish such things entirely. There was always cruelty: it would never be possible to eradicate it altogether. There would also always be poverty. There would always be children who went to bed hungry because their parents could not garner enough food for an evening meal. And there was no wand one could wave to remove the deprivation that could stunt the lives of children, that could swell their bellies with emptiness, while their limbs would be matchstick thin. And then there were the eyes of such children—those saucer-wide eyes that looked out at the world with mute acceptance. There was no pleading, nor anger, because these things asked for energy that simply was not there.

These children, though, currently preparing for a relay race involving twenty teams, were well nourished, thanks to the efforts of Mma Potokwane and the donors she cajoled into supporting the Orphan Farm. She was a warrior, thought Mma Ramotswe; Mma Potokwane was a warrior who went out every day to do battle for these children.

They watched a group of younger children line up for a race. They were milling around and chattering while the starter tried to get them to the start line. And then a shout set them off, like a flock of twittering birds taking off from a field.

"There are some good runners there," remarked Mma Ramotswe.

"That boy in the front is very strong," said Mma Potokwane. "He is from Lobatse, that one. His mother is late and he was being looked after by a grandmother. She became blind, though—that macular . . ."

"Macular degeneration," Mma Ramotswe supplied. "It is very common."

"Yes," said Mma Potokwane. "The grandmother could not see any longer. She could not cook. She could not watch over that little boy. He came to us because there was nobody else."

The race came to an end. The boy from Lobatse threw his hands up in triumph.

"And that one?" said Mma Ramotswe, pointing to another small boy. He had tripped and fallen well short of the finish line and was gingerly examining his grazed knee.

"He's one I worry about a bit," said Mma Potokwane. "His housemother is keeping a good eye on him, but she says that he often cries at night."

"Why is he here, Mma?"

"His father is in prison," Mma Potokwane said. "He was a car thief and they caught him eventually. I have no time for car thieves but they have children, you know, and that particular car thief had eight children. Would you believe that, Mma? He had eight children by different women. He was sent to prison for six years because he had many previous convictions—all for stealing cars. They should have sent him to prison for having all those children by so many different women. And then doing nothing to help look after them, of course."

"There are many men who do not face up to their responsibilities," said Mma Ramotswe. "The government should publish a list of their names so that women could have nothing to do with them."

Mma Potokwane agreed. "There are many things the government should do," she said. "It is hard for them, of course. I'm sure that government ministers come into their office, take one look at their desks, and wonder why they stood for parliament. They will have very long lists of things they have to do."

Mma Ramotswe laughed. "They should have somebody like Mma Makutsi in the government. She would go into those offices and say, 'Have you done this yet? Have you done that?' The ministers would not dare to argue with her. They would say, 'I shall do that right away, Mma.'"

"If women ran countries, Mma Ramotswe," said Mma Potokwane, a wistful note in her voice, "there would be much less trouble in the world. Women don't like wars, for example. They don't like to invade their neighbours, do they? Women don't try to show other people how strong they are."

This brought a sigh. "Oh, Mma, you are so right."

Mma Ramotswe looked over at the boy who had tripped. "And that boy's mother?" she asked. "You say that the father is in prison. What about the mother?"

Mma Potokwane hesitated. "I don't like to blame people for what they are," she said. "Often people are what they are because they have no choice, or because of what has happened to them. But I'm afraid that his mother is not much good. She is a bar lady. She picks up men in a bar down by the bus station. That's during the week. At weekends she goes to a bar called the Go-Go Handsome Man's Bar—you may have heard of it."

Mma Ramotswe recalled that Charlie used to talk of it sometimes, although now that he was married she believed it was out of bounds.

"She probably had to do that just to get by," said Mma Potokwane. "I heard that there was some man from Mahalapye who was living off her earnings. She was probably frightened of him—these poor women often are. But think of it, Mma. Think how dangerous that sort of thing is now. So many people have died. And, of course, she couldn't look after her child. When the social welfare people found the child, he was staying with an aunt from Kanye. But she was already looking after six children under the age of six—two of them were hers, but the others were various waifs and strays—and she was at the end of her tether. Her husband is a taxi driver and he doesn't sleep very well. Having all those young children in a two-bedroom house was not helping him. He had a bad accident when he fell asleep at the wheel and the police said that if it happened again they would take his taxi licence away from him. We took four of the children off her hands—two of them were the children of the same mother and we wanted to keep them together."

"It sounds as if he's better off here, Mma."

Mma Potokwane agreed.

"May I go and speak to him, Mma?" asked Mma Ramotswe.

Mma Potokwane said that she was welcome to do that. She herself had to attend to something elsewhere, and she would leave Mma Ramotswe to speak to the boy. "He's shy, Mma," she said. "But he has good manners."

Mma Ramotswe wondered where those good manners came from? From the mother who earned her living meeting men in bars? From the taxi driver's wife? Or from somewhere else altogether—some natural reservoir of goodness, somewhere within ourselves, from which we could draw if only we were shown how? That was the curious thing about human goodness, Mma Ramotswe thought: it was there, even if everything on the outside seemed stacked against it.

HE LOOKED UP at Mma Ramotswe, but only briefly, as his eyes returned to his bare knee, dusty with its fresh graze. Small droplets of blood made a jagged line on the skin.

Mma Ramotswe dropped to her haunches to inspect the injury. "Let me look at it," she said. "Let Mma see."

The boy winced as she touched the skin lightly. "It is very sore," he said.

"I'm sure it is," said Mma Ramotswe. "Knees are always sore

when you land on them—particularly if you land on stones—which you've done here, I think."

She stood up. "We can go and get a plaster put on this. We can ask Mma Potokwane. She has a big box of plasters in her office—I have seen it."

The boy nodded. "Thank you, Mma."

Mma Ramotswe reached down and put a hand on his shoulder. "You need to tell me your name, I think."

"I am Thabiso."

She clapped her hands together. "Thabiso! I know many people who are called that. They are all very big strong men. It is a good name, I think."

The boy hesitated, and then smiled shyly. "I am going to be strong when I grow up, Mma."

"Of course you will be," said Mma Ramotswe. "I can tell that. But I can also tell that you will be a very polite person too. You can always tell."

The boy looked down at the ground. He was silent.

"I'm sorry you fell over," said Mma Ramotswe.

"I was hoping I would win," said Thabiso. "I have never won a prize, Mma. I was hoping to win today."

"That's a pity," said Mma Ramotswe.

Thabiso looked up at her. He was fiddling with the hem of his shorts. "May I go now, Mma?" he said.

"Yes, of course you may go, Thabiso. But I think you should get Mma Potokwane to wash your knee and put a plaster on it."

"I will do that, Mma."

He turned away. She stopped him.

"Thabiso."

"Yes?"

"Sometimes there is more than one prize, you know."

He frowned.

"I mean," said Mma Ramotswe, "that there are other prizes you may not know about."

He continued to look confused.

She reached out to take his hand. It is so small, she thought. "These are for other things, because often it's not just the person who runs the fastest who deserves a prize. There are prizes for all sorts of other things."

He was staring at her hand, which was covering his own.

"For being brave. There are prizes for that. For not crying when you graze your knee—sometimes there are prizes for that. For being polite. I have heard of prizes being given for that. For helping. There are all sorts of prizes." She paused. "Would you like to win a prize, Thabiso?"

For a few moments he was silent. Then he said, "I would like that very much, Mma."

She reached into the pocket of her blouse and took out a folded fifty-pula note. It was not a large sum, but to a child, particularly this child, it would be a great deal.

She slipped it into his hand. "That is a prize for you, Thabiso. It could be for a lot of things, perhaps, but I think we shall say it is for being brave."

He stared at the money. She wanted to hug him, but she was afraid he might be embarrassed, as small boys can be by such things.

He thanked her. "I am very happy, Mma. I am very happy that I have a prize."

"Good," said Mma Ramotswe. "Now you should go off to get Mma Potokwane to put a plaster on your knee."

She watched him run off. She looked up at the sky. There were so many people, she thought, who deserved a fifty-pula prize, not only for their bravery, but for their patience, their devotion to duty, their doing what they had to do without complaint. The problem was that it would be impossible to give everybody the prizes they deserved. You could make a start, though, with a small prize for a small boy who had faced difficulties in his young life, but who was trying his best. It was a start, and the late Obed Ramotswe, her father, whom she loved so much, always said there were some things you could start even if you knew you might not be able to finish them. He was right about so much, and he was right about this. There was no disgrace in having to give up on something if you had no alternative—what mattered was that you had bothered to try.

AFTER THE SPORTS ENDED, Mma Potokwane invited Mma Ramotswe to join her for a cup of tea in her office.

"The housemothers will be feeding the children now," she said as they made their way back from the playing field. "They work up such an appetite when they run around."

"Energy," mused Mma Ramotswe. "Where does it come from, Mma Potokwane? Even the smallest children have all that energy in them. It always amazes me."

Mma Potokwane smiled. "It is something called metabolism, Mma. Our bodies convert the food we eat into energy for the muscles. That is how it works." She paused. A dove sitting on an acacia branch was watching them, looking down with its tiny black eyes, its head moving with the jerkiness that is a feature of the movement of birds.

Mma Ramotswe considered this explanation. "But if you or I eat something," she said, "do we get the same amount of energy as one of the children will get from the same thing? If I eat a piece of cake, for instance, I don't start to run around as they do if they have a piece of cake of the same size." She paused. "It doesn't seem to work that way."

It was as if Mma Potokwane had addressed that question many times before. Her answer was delivered immediately, and she spoke with the air of one backed by science. "When I was training as a nurse, Mma, all those years ago, we were taught about how people's systems work in different ways. We burn food up inside us at a different rate when we are young. Then, when we are older, we store more of the energy as fat, I'm sorry to say, Mma." She looked at Mma Ramotswe apologetically. "I am not just thinking of traditionally built people like us, Mma. I am thinking of other people too. Everybody has some fat somewhere or other. Some people have it inside them. They are full of fat, Mma, in the inner spaces."

Mma Ramotswe closed her eyes. She did not like to think of such things, and she rather regretted raising the topic with Mma Potokwane. She made an effort to divert the discussion. "It is rather warm today, don't you think, Mma? And we have been out in the sun rather a long time."

But Mma Potokwane was not to be distracted from science. "Then there are people who store their fat on the outside," she continued. "Not outside their skins, of course—that would be very strange—but just under the skin. These are well-padded people. They can sit comfortably for many hours because they have substantial rears, Mma Ramotswe. I do not mean to be rude, but we all know such people. We can always tell who they are when they are walking in front of us."

"Cake," said Mma Ramotswe. "When I mentioned cake, I wasn't talking about your cake in particular, but now that I come to think of it, I can just see a piece of your very delicious cake, Mma—in my mind's eye, of course. There is nobody who makes fruit cake like you do, Mma Potokwane. You are the expert in that department, without any doubt at all. That is well known, I think."

Mma Potokwane was not averse to compliments, and now she thanked her friend for her kindness. "I have always been glad that you enjoy my cake," she said. "Sometimes I offer it to people and they shake their heads and say, 'No.' I cannot understand such people."

Mma Ramotswe sighed. "There are some people who do not know what they are missing—not just when it comes to your fruit cake, Mma, but in a whole lot of other ways. People who have never seen Botswana, for example. Those people do not know what they are missing."

Mma Potokwane agreed. "It is very sad that there are so many people who do not know about Botswana. When these people die, I think, they may wake up in heaven and think, Oh, I am in Botswana."

Mma Ramotswe laughed. "Maybe, Mma. Maybe."

They were nearing the office, and now Mma Ramotswe said, "Isn't it odd, Mma Potokwane, how watching other people doing physical things makes you hungry. You don't have to be doing anything very much yourself, and yet your stomach thinks you have been very busy."

Mma Potokwane smiled. "Oh yes, Mma. Our stomachs always have opinions."

They made their way through the front door of the low building in which Mma Potokwane had her office. This had a shady verandah on two sides—a feature of older local architecture that was often absent from more modern buildings, which were defiantly unshaded in their design. Mma Ramotswe had views on that: the whole point of a building was to protect one from the elements and in particular, if you lived in a warm country, from the sun. In Botswana there were few days of the year when the sun did not appear to be on duty. At times the sky would cloud over, but such conditions would rarely last for long before the sun would reappear. And in winter, when the air might be cold, with the dryness that came with the proximity of the Kalahari, the sun could still be warm enough to make you look for a bit of shade.

But it was not the cold season, and Mma Ramotswe felt immediately more comfortable once they were under the eaves of Mma Potokwane's verandah. And in the office itself, where blinds had been pulled down to block any direct sunlight that might penetrate the windows, there was a delightful coolness.

Mma Potokwane invited her friend to sit down while she filled the kettle and laid a tray with two cups and saucers. Mma Ramotswe found her gaze falling on the shelf behind the matron's desk. The battered round tin, with its ancient inscription, *Peek Frean's Biscuits*, was in its accustomed place. Although it may once have contained pink iced wafers and small squares of shortbread, this tin had long been given over to even more delicious and irresistible contents: the fruit cake for which Mma Potokwane was renowned. Of her many talents, the ability to bake near-perfect fruit cake was the one that Mma Ramotswe most admired. She had been given the recipe by Mma Potokwane, who, unlike some bakers, was generous in these matters, but Mma Ramotswe's efforts to replicate the fruit cake had somehow failed. She had followed the recipe closely but there had been something lacking in the cake she made. Mr. J.L.B. Matekoni had been polite—he always was—and had said that it was every bit as delicious as anything made by Mma Potokwane, but she had been able to tell that he was saying this only so as not to hurt her feelings.

"You can be honest about this cake," she said to him. "You can say what you really think, Rra. That is one of the good things about being married, I think. You can tell the truth about your wife's cake."

Mr. J.L.B. Matekoni had taken another bite, just to be sure. Then he had sighed. "It is true that there is something lacking, Mma.

I did not want to say it, but there is." He paused. "You are a very good cook—very good. When I think of your beef stew and pumpkin, my mouth waters. Just thinking about it is enough."

She thanked him, and said that perhaps she should stick to the recipes she had always used. "We should not try to be other people," she said. "I am not Mma Potokwane. She is the fruit-cake lady. I am not."

"Well, there you are," said Mr. J.L.B. Matekoni. "All of us are what we are." He reached out and touched her lightly on her forearm. "And I am glad that you are who you are, Mma, and that I am married to you. There is no other lady in Botswana—in the whole country—I would prefer to be married to. Not one."

"And I am glad that I am married to you," she said. "If the president of this country or that country came to me and said, 'Marry me, Mma Ramotswe,' I would say, 'No thank you. I have a far better husband. I am married to Mr. J.L.B. Matekoni of Tlokweng Road Speedy Motors, and that is good enough for me.'"

They were two small and unexpected speeches of loyalty, prompted by reflections on fruit cake, but powerful nonetheless. She returned his touch, laying her hand on the rough khaki fabric of his working shirt. She was content. She would not change a word of what she had said about being married to him, and she knew that he, too, meant every word that he had uttered. Mr. J.L.B. Matekoni was a man of complete truthfulness. He is a good man, she thought, and he is mine. I am the most fortunate woman I know.

But now she was sitting in Mma Potokwane's office, taking the first sip of the cup of red bush tea that Mma Potokwane had prepared for her. Mma Potokwane preferred ordinary tea, although she would occasionally join Mma Ramotswe in a cup of red bush if she felt like a change. They were both strong adherents of the view that any sort of tea was good for you, and that it did not matter how much one drank. "Nobody ever looks back over her life and says, 'I wish I had drunk less tea,'" Mma Ramotswe observed. Nor did one ever hear, at a funeral service, the words, "She drank far too much tea."

Mma Ramotswe took a second sip. Her gaze had been fixed on the Peek Frean's biscuit tin, and now she was struggling with the temptation to turn Mma Potokwane's attention in the same direction. She would have to be careful, though: it was bad manners to ask for something directly, and so she could hardly say, "A slice of fruit cake would be most welcome, Mma," or words to that effect.

But there were indirect ways of making the same point, and so she said, "Have you been busy baking, Mma Potokwane?"

Mma Potokwane answered with a sigh. "There has been so much going on, Mma. I wish I had a few more hours in the day—then I could do the things that I really enjoy doing, such as baking."

This was an unpromising start. Mma Ramotswe found herself wondering whether the tin was empty—a distinct possibility if Mma Potokwane had been too busy to spend much time in the kitchen.

"I know what you mean," she said evenly. "We all have so many demands on our time these days. And yet . . ."

Mma Potokwane raised an eyebrow. "Yes, Mma?"

"And yet, I think it's important that you *make* time for really important things . . . such as baking."

Mma Potokwane nodded her agreement. "You're right, Mma Ramotswe," she said. "We women have so many people coming to us and asking us to do things. We should just say: I cannot do this thing you want me to do because I have . . ."

"To bake a fruit cake," suggested Mma Ramotswe.

"Exactly," said Mma Potokwane. And then, quite unexpectedly, she looked over her shoulder towards the tin. "Oh, my goodness, Mma Ramotswe. I have been so rude. I should have offered you a piece of cake. Here I am sitting and drinking tea and leaving my old friend without so much as a crumb of cake."

Mma Ramotswe struggled to conceal her relief. "You have not been at all rude, Mma," she said. "But, since you ask, I must say that I would very much enjoy a piece of cake . . . if you were to offer it to me."

"Which I shall certainly do," said Mma Potokwane, reaching for the tin. "Here, I shall cut you an especially large piece to make up for my neglect."

She was as good as her word, the slice of cake she offered to Mma Ramotswe being at least three times the size of a normal piece. Mma Ramotswe did not object, but immediately took a bite of the highly regarded confection. "Most delicious," she said. "As always, Mma Potokwane."

They sat in silence for a few moments, savouring the tea and cake, utterly content in one another's company. Then Mma Ramotswe said, "We had a rather unusual visitor in the agency yesterday, as it happens."

Mma Potokwane looked interested. "You are always having interesting clients, Mma. I cannot remember when you last said to me that you had had a dull one. I suppose that's to do with the nature of your business. The people who come through your door are people who have done something unusual. Otherwise, they wouldn't be in trouble."

Mma Ramotswe said that she thought this was broadly true. Then she went on, "This man who came to see us yesterday was not our average client, you know."

"Oh yes?"

"You know, Mma," Mma Ramotswe said, "I don't normally dislike people. You know that, don't you?"

Mma Potokwane nodded. "That is definitely true," she said.

"You are a very tolerant lady, I think. Perhaps even too tolerant at times—I wouldn't put up with what you put up with. I would give people a piece of my mind."

Mma Ramotswe did not like to say it, but that, too, was quite true. Mma Potokwane was not one to be crossed. Now she went on: "This man who came to see us yesterday was a most irritating man, Mma. He was one of those people who just gets under your skin. You know how it is."

"Oh, I do," said Mma Potokwane. "There's a man in the government welfare department who does that to me. The moment he opens his mouth, I find myself wanting to shout at him. The poor man—he can't help it, I think, but I just can't stand him." She paused. "Was your client like that?"

Mma Ramotswe hesitated. Her dislike of Mr. Excellence Modise had not been instant, but had become stronger as their encounter progressed. By the time he left, she found that she was on the verge of showing her irritation openly. "I did not dislike him immediately," she said. "It took a bit of time."

Mma Potokwane nodded. "There are some people who improve the longer you know them," she said. "And then there are others who seem worse every time you see them."

The matron drained her cup, and then enquired as to whether Mma Ramotswe would like more tea. She said that she would.

"Could you tell me," asked Mma Potokwane, as she settled back in her chair, "could you tell me who this irritating person is, Mma?"

"He is called Mr. Excellence Modise," answered Mma Ramotswe.

This brought forth a hoot of laughter from Mma Potokwane. "Oh, Mma, I know exactly who you're talking about. That man! Oh, goodness, he's one of the most annoying men in Botswana—and that's official."

Mma Ramotswe had not expected this, although she realised that she should not be surprised. Botswana was a large country geographically, but the population was small, and this meant that people often knew who others were, or, as was frequently the case, were related to them. In general, it was safest to assume that if you were talking to somebody about another person, they were, in fact, cousins.

"So, you know that man?" she asked.

"Yes," replied Mma Potokwane. "I know that man. His wife is the cousin of a man who comes here to fix the plumbing. The plumber has often spoken about him. He finds him irritating, too, Mma."

It seemed to Mma Ramotswe that this was a rather tenuous connection. "But have you met him yourself?" she asked.

Mma Potokwane nodded. "He came out here one day to speak to us about termite eradication," she said. "He was offering us a contract to deal with our termites. But we don't have many, as it happens, and so I told him that we did not need his services. That didn't seem to put him off. He went on and on about ants, Mma. Ants, ants, ants. He never stopped talking and he made very silly jokes, as I recall. And he repeats words. He says a lot of things twice-twice."

Mma Ramotswe remembered how Excellence had tried to be funny but had failed to amuse Mma Makutsi. "I think he may not realise that his manner irritates people," she said. "Perhaps nobody has told him."

Mma Potokwane looked doubtful. "You are very kind, Mma Ramotswe. You like to see the good in people—even people like Mr. Excellence Modise. But I think he is just a rather irritating man—and that's all there is to it."

Mma Ramotswe was silent for a while. She did not like taking a negative view of people, and she would have liked to say something positive about Excellence Modise—but she was finding it difficult.

Then Mma Potokwane said, "Why did he come to see you, Mma?"

"He is concerned about his wife," said Mma Ramotswe.

"His wife? What about her?"

"He thinks she is having an affair with another man."

Mma Potokwane tried not to laugh. "But wouldn't you have an affair if you were married to a man like that?" she asked. "Poor woman—he's probably driven her to distraction."

Mma Ramotswe looked away. She did not think that Mma Potokwane was serious. Having an annoying husband was no excuse to engage in a clandestine affair. If things were that difficult, a marriage could be ended with dignity and in such a way as to minimise the hurt caused to the other party. No, Mma Potokwane could not be serious.

Seeing the effect of her remark, Mma Potokwane said, "I'm sorry, Mma. I wasn't thinking. I would never say that Mma Modise had no alternative but to run off with another man. No, I would not say that. All I would say is that I can understand how hard it must be for her to have a husband like Excellence. That's all, Mma."

Mma Ramotswe assured Mma Potokwane that she did not think she had been intemperate. "People can be very difficult," she said. "And in this case, I have been thinking of getting in touch with this man and telling him I cannot help him after all."

Her tone was apologetic, and she was watching for Mma Potokwane's reaction. But the matron seemed unperturbed. "You can't help everybody, Mma Ramotswe," she said. "People can't think that they can just walk into your office and be helped with all their problems." She paused. "Especially if those problems are their own fault."

Mma Ramotswe frowned. "But I'm not sure, Mma, whether Mr. Excellence Modise's problems *are* his fault. Can he help it if his wife is having an affair with another man?"

Mma Potokwane considered this. Domestic discord, she thought, was usually caused by all sorts of factors—all operating together. It was rarely a simple matter. But in this case, having seen how irritating Mr. Excellence Modise was, she felt that it was likely that he had brought the whole situation upon himself. "I'm sorry, Mma," she said. "But you can't help everybody. You need not feel guilty if you tell this man that the No. 1 Ladies' Detective Agency is unable to help him."

Mma Ramotswe looked into her teacup. Life was not as simple as Mma Potokwane sometimes suggested it was. And now, in a rather unexpected way, she found herself feeling sorry for Mr. Excellence Modise, in spite of everything. To be disliked by one's spouse was a hard sentence to bear, although . . . Suddenly she experienced a moment of doubt. Was Mr. Excellence Modise telling the truth? She had not asked herself that question before now, but it came to her, and she felt unsettled. In her profession, she had at various times felt a strong suspicion that a client was lying. It had not happened very often, but the interesting thing is that when this doubt had occurred, it had always subsequently proved to be well founded. In fact, she had never been wrong about this—not once.

She raised the possibility guiltily. "It's possible that he may not be telling me the truth," she said. "I don't know why I should think that, but I must admit that I feel that way."

Mma Potokwane's response to this was robust. "Of course he's lying," she said. "That sort of man is full of hot air. When he was trying to get me to sign one of his ridiculous termite contracts, he said all sorts of things about ants that were clearly not true. He wanted me to think that there were whole armies of ants planning an invasion of the Orphan Farm. Did I believe him? I did not, Mma Ramotswe. Most ants have got better things to do than to spend their time plotting against these poor children." She fixed Mma Ramotswe with a bemused stare. Then she continued, "You are a very kind lady, Mma Ramotswe. Sometimes, I think you are too kind. If you don't want to help this man, then you don't have to." She paused. "But why would he be lying, Mma? Can you think of any reason for a man to tell you that his wife is having an affair when she isn't?"

Mma Ramotswe took a sip of her tea and glanced at her watch. She would need to start the journey back to town if she was to have time to pick up a few things at the shops at River Walk. "Sometimes people imagine things," she said. "They call it paranoia, I believe. It is like an infection—a cold that doesn't go away—except that it's all in the person's mind. You think that people are doing things that they aren't really doing. You think that people are against you."

"So, this might make him think his wife does not like him?" Mma Potokwane asked.

"Possibly."

Mma Potokwane looked thoughtful. "But in this case," she said, "there is every reason to think that he's right. We don't like him, and so it's more likely than not that she doesn't like him either. And if she doesn't like him, then that would be a reason for her to go off and find a man whom she *does* like. And I'm afraid that leads to a difficult question, Mma: Whose side should you be on?"

Mma Ramotswe frowned. There could be only one answer to that question, she thought: she should be on the side of the client. That was at the heart of her profession, as Clovis Andersen himself pointed out in *The Principles of Private Detection* when he wrote: *Remember that it is your duty to stand by your client. That is a matter of professional ethics and is non-negotiable. Personal feelings should not come into it.* And yet, and yet . . . What if Mr. Excellence Modise's wife was miserable in her marriage? Why should she, Mma Ramotswe, act to prolong the poor woman's unhappiness?

She would have to think about it further, she said. Sometimes problems like this seemed different after one had slept on them for a few days. She suggested this to Mma Potokwane, and the matron said that she was of that view too—although there were times when sleeping on a problem made it seem even bigger the next morning. "I expect, though, that in this case you are going to do what you always do, Mma Ramotswe."

Mma Ramotswe waited.

"Which is to ignore the fact that Mr. Excellence Modise is an extremely annoying man."

"Well . . ."

"No, I am sure of it," said Mma Potokwane. "You will help that man, and you are right to do so, Mma. You must forget what I said about telling him to go away. That is not the way your heart wants you to go, I think."

Mma Ramotswe looked at her friend. This was the advice that she had secretly hoped for, and she inclined her head in acceptance. And inclined it again when Mma Potokwane suggested that before she left, she would wrap up a piece of cake for her to take home with her.

"Cake always helps," she said. "But you know that, don't you?"

Mma Ramotswe did. "I shall take this back home to give to the children," she said. "Puso loves your cake, Mma—as does Motholeli. They are hoping one day that you will teach them how to bake it for themselves."

"I shall be happy to do that, Mma Ramotswe," said Mma Potokwane.

Mma Potokwane came with her to the door. "Have you got a moment, Mma?" she asked as they stood on the verandah. "I would like to show you something I am growing." She pointed in the direction of the small vegetable garden behind the office. "I have been working hard, Mma. I have some very promising pumpkins."

"Pumpkins!"

Mma Potokwane smiled. "I knew you'd be interested. They're not ready, of course, but when they are, oh, my goodness, they will be the number one pumpkins in the Tlokweng Agricultural Show. These are *competitive* pumpkins, you see, Mma."

They went together to the patch of garden, where Mma Ramotswe was shown the pumpkin vines with their promising fruit.

"Those are very fine indeed," said Mma Ramotswe. "You are a very fortunate woman, Mma."

"I know," said Mma Potokwane.

She spoke without any suggestion of self-satisfaction or smugness. She *was* fortunate, and she did not feel that she had to conceal the fact. She was fortunate to be who she was, living where she was, and doing what she did. She was fortunate to be able to spend time with a friend like Mma Ramotswe, drinking tea, talking about matters of the day, and having a slice—or two—of cake at the same time. She was fortunate to have this little patch of garden on which to grow a few pumpkins of such . . . of such *status*. These were all fine things, as Mma Ramotswe so rightly said.

She looked fondly at her friend, who would shortly be getting into her tiny white van and driving back down the road to Gaborone, just a few miles away.

"Please come back soon," she said.

Mma Ramotswe smiled. That was the best sort of farewell, she thought. *Please come back soon.* And she replied, "I shall, Mma Potokwane. I shall come back soon."

CHAPTER THREE

LISTEN TO YOUR SHOES

"WE ARE TWO very different businesses in one," Mma Ramotswe was fond of saying. "But we are also two businesses that are very similar. On one side we cater for cars—and the things that go wrong with cars—and on the other, we look after people—and the things that go wrong with people."

Broadly speaking, this was true. Tlokweng Road Speedy Motors was, as the name suggested, a garage, and the No. 1 Ladies' Detective Agency was, also as the name suggested, a detective agency run by two ladies and committed to helping people who were encountering some issue in their lives and who, as a result, needed help. Both businesses were therefore caring businesses—concerns to which the mechanically troubled and the otherwise troubled might have recourse.

Both businesses were small. Tlokweng Road Speedy Motors was run by Mr. J.L.B. Matekoni, that great *garagiste*, with the regular assistance of a young mechanic called Fanwell, formerly an apprentice under Mr. J.L.B. Matekoni's direction, and the less frequent assistance of another young man, Charlie. This young man had begun his mechanical apprenticeship at the same time as Fanwell had, but had not completed the theoretical part of the course insisted upon by the Botswana Motor Trades Authority, and was therefore not, strictly speaking, a qualified mechanic. And there were other grounds for distinguishing between these two. Fanwell was cautious: he never forced machinery and he gave his mechanical diagnoses only after careful consideration of all the evidence. In particular he had absorbed the teaching that Mr. J.L.B. Matekoni gave: he understood the importance of listening to what a car's engine had to say.

"An engine will always tell you what is wrong," Mr. J.L.B. Matekoni said. "Engines do not believe in suffering in silence. All you have to do is to listen to what they have to say, and to learn the words that they use."

Charlie had never concealed his amusement over this advice. "The boss goes on about listening to engines," he remarked. "He says they talk. I do not think that is the case. An engine either goes *brum brum* or it is silent because it is not working. That's it. Story over."

Fanwell took a different view. "The boss knows what he's talking about," he said. "If you've been fixing engines as long as the boss has been doing, then you know what they sound like. *Brum brum* may be their normal sound, but what about *brim brim*? What if an engine goes *knock knock*? They do, you know. That's the bearings—every time. You only have to listen."

There had not been enough work for both young men once they had completed their apprenticeship period, and so Mr. J.L.B. Matekoni had, quite properly, offered the one available job to Fanwell, who had at least passed his exams. This had been a very painful decision for him, as he was a sympathetic man, and he did not like the thought of turning Charlie out into the world without a qualification and with no other post to which he might go. That was when Mma Ramotswe, whose heart was every bit as large as Mr. J.L.B. Matekoni's, had come to the rescue and had offered, at some cost to herself, to take Charlie on as an assistant on the agency side. By providing him with part-time work as an apprentice private detective, she made it possible for him to take up her husband's offer of part-time employment in the garage as an unqualified mechanic.

That suited Charlie perfectly. He was happy enough to keep his hand in at the garage, but the idea of being an employee of a detective agency was, in his view, far more glamorous. He leapt at the opportunity that Mma Ramotswe gave him, even if he could hardly miss Mma Makutsi's lack of enthusiasm for his being on the staff of the detective agency. She had initially refused to confer on him any status at all, pointedly referring to him as an office assistant and occasionally even as an assistant office assistant, rather than by the title that he himself preferred: junior detective. She had come round slowly, though, eventually thawing to the point of acknowledging that there were circumstances in which Charlie could be useful enough—"for routine matters, that is."

If Tlokweng Speedy Motors was a small business, then so too was the No. 1 Ladies' Detective Agency. The full complement of staff was two ladies—Mma Ramotswe and Mma Makutsi—and part of Charlie. The agency's premises were similarly restricted in size, consisting of a single room in which there were two desks, two and a half filing cabinets and three chairs: one for Mma Ramotswe, another for Mma Makutsi, and a third for the use of clients. Charlie had no chair, and if he needed to sit down, he was obliged to perch on top of the half-size filing cabinet.

Mma Ramotswe had raised with Mma Makutsi the possibility of getting a chair for Charlie, and possibly a small table, if not a proper office desk.

"It would be nice if he could sit down occasionally," she said to Mma Makutsi. "Everybody needs to sit down from time to time, Mma."

Mma Makutsi was not convinced. "There is very little room in our office," she argued. "If Charlie has a chair, then what will he do with it? He will try to sit down all the time, Mma. That is what happens when you give people a chair—they try to sit down."

Mma Ramotswe had waited for this objection to be expanded upon, but there had been nothing more, and the matter was dropped. Privately, though, she had explained to Charlie that there was a shortage of space in the office, and that although she would like to give him somewhere to sit, it was not possible to do so—just yet.

"You are very kind, Mma Ramotswe," the young man said. "I would like to have a chair one day, but I am not unhappy standing up. And I can sit down on the filing cabinet if I want to. It is not too uncomfortable."

Mma Ramotswe appreciated his understanding. "You are a very uncomplaining young man," she said. "People like that quality. People don't like moaners."

Charlie nodded. "Like Mma Makutsi, Mma. She is a big moaner, isn't she?"

Mma Ramotswe had not let him get away with that. "Mma Makutsi is not just anybody, Charlie. She is an equal partner with me in this business, and you must not call your employers moaners."

"I am not calling *you* that," said Charlie. "You are not going on about this thing and that thing all the time. Not you, Mma Ramotswe. I am referring to a certain Mma Makutsi, who thinks she's Miss Big Time Special because she got ninety-two per cent or whatever it was at the Botswana Secretarial College. That is who I'm talking about."

"Ninety-*seven* per cent," Mma Ramotswe corrected. "And I do not want you to pick a fight with Mma Makutsi, Charlie. This is a happy office and we all get on with one another very well—all the time."

Such exchanges had not been infrequent at the beginning of Charlie's career in the agency, but they had become much rarer as time went by. And in due course, the unwelcoming attitude that Mma Makutsi showed to Charlie was replaced by an attitude of greater tolerance and, eventually, what might even be described as affection.

"I have to admit that Charlie is making progress," Mma Makutsi observed to Mma Ramotswe while Charlie was out of the office on some errand. "It's interesting, isn't it, Mma, how young men grow out of their earlier nonsense and become more responsible. I have read somewhere that this is because when they are younger, men's brains are all mixed up and need time to sort themselves out. They are like a big jumble of wires and fuses and so on, but they become a bit more like women's brains as they get older. I have read all about that, Mma. This is something called neuroscience."

Mma Ramotswe had listened to this and expressed cautious agreement. "It is very hard for young men," she said. "They need time. And yes, Charlie is much less headstrong than he used to be. He is doing very well, and I am glad that you are becoming so fond of him, Mma."

"Not *so* fond," Mma Makutsi said quickly. "A *bit* fond, perhaps. You are right, though: Charlie is less . . . less like he used to be. But there is still room for improvement."

ON THAT PARTICULAR AFTERNOON, while Mma Ramotswe was out at Tlokweng, watching the sports at the Orphan Farm and subsequently having tea with Mma Potokwane, the premises of Tlokweng Road Speedy Motors and the No. 1 Ladies' Detective Agency, if not actually somnolent in the afternoon heat, were nonetheless quieter than usual. On the garage side, Fanwell had been sent off to attend a refresher course in automotive hydraulics—a subject that Mr. J.L.B. Matekoni had never enjoyed but that needed to be understood by at least one member of the garage staff. Charlie, although he would normally have been on duty if Fanwell was away, had requested and been given the afternoon off to attend a family gathering of his wife's people: an aunt, recently widowed, had found a prospective new husband, who had come down from Palapye to meet his possible new relatives. Delicate property negotiations were involved, as the new husband was comfortably off and had avaricious children. Both sides wanted to be represented in the largest possible numbers, to give weight to their respective family positions, and so Charlie had been inveigled into attending. That left only Mr. J.L.B. Matekoni in attendance at the garage, which did not matter particularly, as there was little, if anything, to do. There had been a couple of cars in for servicing, but this had been a simple matter of changing oil and filters, checking batteries, and attending to one or two minor electrical issues. This had all been done before lunch, with the result that there seemed to be nothing left to do during the long, warm hours of the afternoon.

On the agency side, Mma Makutsi was at her desk, but was giving serious consideration to closing the office for the afternoon. There had been a few things to do that morning—including making a trip to the bank and to the stationery store, but once that was done, Mma Makutsi could think of nothing that had to be done. She was up to date with her filing—indeed she was more than up to date, having reclassified some of the aged files and weeded out unnecessary material from others. These were highly skilled tasks, in Mma Makutsi's opinion, which she alone was qualified to perform. She had received a particular commendation for filing at the end of that module of her secretarial course, and had been described by the tutor as being "arguably the best filer ever to have attended the college." That commendation had meant so much, but had unfortunately only been a verbal one. If only, thought Mma Makutsi, it had been written down somewhere, it could have been given the prominence it deserved—but this was not to be.

Mma Ramotswe filed papers occasionally, although Mma Makutsi wished that she would not. She could not stop her, of course, as technically the business belonged to her, but Mma Makutsi had nonetheless discouraged her from interfering. "I have a very good system, Mma Ramotswe," she had said. "In general, it is better, in the world of filing, for one person—and I mean one *qualified* person—to attend to all the filing, even if there are others who, quite naturally, want to be as helpful as possible." There had then come a pause that had hung heavily in the air for almost a full minute. This was followed by, "There's a reason for this, you see. People may think that they know which file a letter should go into, but they may have it wrong. As a result, a letter, for instance, may be put into the file pertaining to its sender, whereas the correct procedure might be to put it in the file pertaining to its *subject*. There is a difference there, you see. A sender is one thing, and a subject is another. There is a very important distinction that some people—and I am not suggesting that you are one of them, Mma Ramotswe—would not grasp. I am just giving that as an example. There are many others."

Without any filing to do, with no letters to be opened, and with no reports to write, the afternoon stretched out in front of Mma Makutsi. She toyed with the idea of locking up and going home, but tempting though that was, she had assured Mma Ramotswe that she would be there until she returned from Tlokweng and she did not want to let her down. Inevitably, when the office was closed during normal working hours, somebody would arrive without an appointment, and business might be lost. So she sat back in her chair and opened a magazine that she had been saving for just such a moment. The magazine was engaging. There were several articles on home decoration, with excellent ideas, she thought, and a long first-person piece about a woman who took secret driving lessons in the face of her husband's opposition. Mma Makutsi was surprised that any husband these days should imagine he had the right to stop his wife from learning to drive. She read the article with a growing sense of indignation, and was pleased when, in the final paragraph, the wife passed her driving test with what was described as "an almost perfect score of almost one hundred per cent." The precise figure was not mentioned, and Mma Makutsi momentarily speculated as to whether it was above ninety-seven per cent, or below it. Probably below, she decided, but it was impressive nonetheless.

She listened for sounds coming from the garage. When Fanwell or Charlie were working with Mr. J.L.B. Matekoni, a radio could often be heard in the background, playing the sort of music that the two young men enjoyed but that she knew Mr. J.L.B. Matekoni did not particularly like. It all seemed so much the same to her—an endless beat that never seemed to be going anywhere. Now there was silence, although it was punctuated from time to time by the ringing of Mr. J.L.B. Matekoni's phone and the sound of ensuing, business-like conversations. She looked at her watch. In fifteen minutes or so, she would go through to the garage and announce that tea was ready. Until then, there was the magazine, and, in particular, her horoscope to look at. Not that she believed in such nonsense, but it was always entertaining to see what the stars had in store for one, even though there might be no point in paying any attention to their predictions.

You are in for a big surprise, said the resident astrologist. Well, thought Mma Makutsi, that was hardly very helpful. We were *all* in for big surprises, given the state of the world. What would be truly surprising would be if there were no surprises.

You will meet a new person, the column continued. *Always be open to new experiences, but remember to be cautious. Not everybody you encounter on life's journey wishes you well. Old friends and acquaintances are always best.*

Mma Makutsi frowned, and read the prediction once more. *Not everybody you encounter on life's journey wishes you well.* That was undoubtedly true, as a moment's thought would surely confirm. She wondered whether the warning was a general one—or whether it was specific to some person whom she was about to encounter. And as for old friends and acquaintances—that must refer to people like Mma Ramotswe and Mr. J.L.B. Matekoni. On that subject, the caster of the horoscope was undoubtedly correct. Friends like that were irreplaceable.

She lowered the magazine with a smile. Horoscopes were harmless enough, perhaps, but there was really little point in reading them. So she laid the magazine aside and looked up at the ceiling. It was at this point that she heard the sound of voices in the garage. She strained to make out what was being said. Mr. J.L.B. Matekoni was talking to somebody, but it was clear neither what he was saying nor to whom he was talking. There was another voice, but not one she recognised. It was certainly neither Fanwell nor Charlie. *This was a new person . . .*

Mma Makutsi rose from her desk and crossed the floor. The door that led into the garage was closed, masking the sound of voices beyond, but by crouching down and putting an ear to the door panels she was able to hear a little bit more clearly. That was Mr. J.L.B. Matekoni talking—saying something about a car—and that was the other person, a man. The visitors said something about having to go somewhere—Francistown, was it? Or was it Lobatse? Then Mr. J.L.B. Matekoni said that there would have to be rain soon and that the weather surely could not get any hotter.

The handle of the door turned—somebody on the other side was preparing to open it. Mma Makutsi moved back guiltily: it would not do to be caught listening at doors, even if the door at which one was listening was the door to one's own office.

The door opened, and Mma Makutsi, who had picked up a file and was paging through its contents with what she hoped was an expression of convincing attention, looked up in what she hoped would be taken as surprise.

"Ah, Mr. J.L.B. Matekoni," she said. "What a surprise."

It was not a surprise, of course, and he pointed this out to her. "You must have been expecting me, Mma. After all, I do work here."

Mma Makutsi gave a shrill laugh. "Of course you do, Rra. It's just that I was so busy with this case that my thoughts were somewhere else altogether."

Mr. J.L.B. Matekoni smiled. "But not so far away as to be unable to make tea for our guest here, Mma." He turned and gestured to the man at his side. Mma Makutsi shot a glance at the other man. His face was familiar, but only, she thought, because it was unexceptional.

"You may be wondering who I am, Mma," said the man. "I am Mr. Freddie Mogorosi."

Mma Makutsi reached out to take the hand offered in greeting. "How are you, Rra?"

"I am very well, thank you, Mma."

Mr. J.L.B. Matekoni said that Mr. Mogorosi had just arrived after a dusty journey and would undoubtedly appreciate a cup of tea.

"Strong, and without milk," said Mr. Mogorosi. "Ladies are always trying to get men to drink weak tea, and we are always saying that we do not want that sort of thing."

"I am glad that you yourself seem to resist," said Mr. J.L.B. Matekoni. "The world is full of people who are incapable of standing up for themselves. They must be encouraged to resist."

Mma Makutsi glanced at Mr. J.L.B. Matekoni. This was a rather out-of-character remark for him, she thought. He was the mildest of men, and she found it hard to imagine him rallying these legions of weak people who failed to stand up for themselves. Was he saying this, she wondered, to impress Mr. Mogorosi?

She smiled. "At least you know where you stand, Mr. J.L.B. Matekoni," she said. "You know what sort of tea you want in this life."

Mr. Mogorosi found this amusing. "Oh, very good, Mma." And to Mr. J.L.B. Matekoni he said, "I can see that your secretary knows what's what, Rra."

Twice in a short period of time had this grave solecism been uttered—first, by Mr. Excellence Modise in the course of his interview with Mma Ramotswe, and now by Mr. Freddie Mogorosi in this ill-thought-out throwaway remark. And while Mma Makutsi was prepared to bite her tongue on one occasion, it was simply too much to expect her to do this again so soon after the commission of the original offence. She stood rooted to the spot, near the filing cabinet on the top of which the tea tray and the kettle were kept. Turning to Mr. Mogorosi, she said, "I am a fully qualified private detective, Rra. I am not a secretary." And then she added, for good measure, just in case he might not appreciate the gravity of the offence he had caused, "Not every woman whom you find in an office, Rra, is a secretary, you know. Some women in offices are the boss—or, as in this particular case, the executive president for business development."

Mr. J.L.B. Matekoni frowned. "Executive president for development? Who is an executive president for development? I have never heard of such a person."

Mma Makutsi glared at him. "I am the executive president for development in the No. 1 Ladies' Detective Agency. This is my official position."

Mr. J.L.B. Matekoni shrugged. "That's the first I've heard of that, Mma. But if that is what you are, then of course that is what you are." And then he added, rather lamely, but with real feeling, "Sorry, Mma Makutsi. I really didn't know. I am just a mechanic, you see. Mechanics don't always know these things."

Mr. Freddie Mogorosi looked bemused. "Do titles mean much, Mma? Surely, it's what you do that counts. People can call themselves what they like these days. They can make up any sort of title. Even the Pope. You want to call yourself the Pope, there's nothing in the law of Botswana, as far as I'm aware, that's stopping you. And if the Pope wants to call himself executive president for something or other, then he can do just that."

If he intended this to be conciliatory, it had the opposite effect. Tight-lipped, Mma Makutsi made three cups of tea. When she handed one to Mr. Mogorosi, she did so without saying anything, ignoring his elaborate thank-you. Returning to her desk, she busied herself with a sheaf of papers, studiously avoiding making any eye contact with their visitor. Sensing her disapproval, Mr. J.L.B. Matekoni proposed that he and Mr. Mogorosi should drink their tea outside, where it was now considerably cooler.

Mma Makutsi sat at her desk, inwardly fuming. "Stupid man," she muttered. She had not liked him. It was not just his tactless remark about her being a secretary—she could forgive that mistake in normal circumstances, even if it was irritating. No, it was not that; it was something deeper. This man was dishonest. He was untrustworthy. Anybody could see that.

And somebody had. For at that moment, she heard a small voice, faint and distant, a voice that seemed to come from somewhere altogether elsewhere—the sort of voice that might belong to a tiny, scurrying creature; the sort of voice that might be no more than the sound of the wind in a corner, but distinct enough for all that. *That man,* whispered the voice. *Bad news, if you ask us, Boss.*

She looked down. Her shoes were half concealed under her desk.

"What?" she said.

The shoes looked back up at her from their darkness, unblinking. They were quiet. They were impassive. They had nothing further to say. If people would not listen to their shoes, then what could they do?

CHAPTER FOUR

WE ARE A BIT LIKE ANTS

MMA RAMOTSWE had intended to return to the office after her visit to Mma Potokwane, but a number of small errands demanded to be done, and these kept her busy until shortly before five o'clock in the afternoon. By that stage there would be no point in her going into the office, only to leave for home a few minutes later. So, rather than do that, she embarked on her final task of the day—the purchase of groceries for that evening's dinner, and for the weekend ahead. It was already Friday, and the week seemed to have gone so quickly. But that, she felt, was how time now went—with a fleetness that she would love somehow to arrest, but that she knew was beyond her control. "Have you noticed how time seems to be speeding up?" she had once asked Mma Makutsi. And Mma Makutsi, after a few moments' reflection, had replied, "Or we are slowing down, Mma."

It had been a thought-provoking remark, and the more she mulled it over, as she did now as she found a parking spot near the supermarket, the more she realised that Mma Makutsi was probably right. She had not paid attention to the subject in the past, but then there were many things that one did not really dwell upon until one became a bit older, as we all inevitably did. Not that Mma Ramotswe regarded herself as middle-aged—she was not—as far as she was concerned. Middle age began when . . . She paused as she asked herself the uncomfortable question. The answer was that middle age began not just yet. Mma Potokwane was almost middle-aged, perhaps, but that was because Mma Potokwane was in her late forties, a few years older than Mma Ramotswe—or at least *one* year older, possibly more—and if you were in your late forties, then it might be said that you were closer to fifty than to forty. And if you were fifty, then the next big milestone was definitely in the middle-aged bracket. And thereafter, it was time to start thinking of finding a chair somewhere in a sunny place and sitting in it while you watched the world go past. That, though, was a long, long time away, and for the time being there were rather immediate decisions to be made—such as whether to get some mince to make a pie for dinner that night—Mr. J.L.B. Matekoni regarded pies as something of a treat—a rather middle-aged preference, perhaps—although he also enjoyed stew, or sausages with fried potatoes and pumpkin. You could never go wrong with pumpkin, she felt, as it could be served up to anybody and be greeted, in just about every case, with a smile of welcome. It was possible that there were people who did not like pumpkin, but Mma Ramotswe had never encountered anybody who turned their nose up at pumpkins or the sweeter variety of *tsamma* melons, such as the *senwane*, that could be made into jam or used to slake thirst.

She opened the door of her van and emerged into the late afternoon sunlight. All about her, there was movement and activity, as shoppers—engaged, like her, on a quest for supplies for the evening meal—made their way across the car park to the cool sanctuary of the supermarket. *We are a bit like ants*, she thought, and smiled. Ants can sense where supplies of food are, and will troop in tiny lines across what must be, to them, great plains and deserts—to us, just small stretches of ground—to whatever food their acute sense of smell had detected: a scrap dropped by some passer-by; or some small creature that has died on its own quest for food and would soon become a feast for the lesser life living down among the grains of sand; the manna of a piece of fallen fruit.

All these creatures, Precious, are our brothers and sisters, you know. All of them . . . That was what her father had said to her. Those were the exact words that he used when he would take her for walks through the bush and show her the things that he thought it important for her to see. He would give her the Setswana words for the creatures they came across—even the small, scurrying beetles—and it was only later that she realised why he had done this. It was because he wanted her to value and take delight in nature, and it was harder, much harder, to be unkind to anything once you knew the Setswana word for it. That was what he sensed—and he was so right. Of course he was right. If you knew the Setswana word for an insignificant little creature, you understood where it stood in the order of things, and you *felt* for it. That was her father's insight, even if she had never realised it at the time, although she did later on. And thinking of it now, she glanced up at the sky, which was something she often did when she thought of her father, the late Obed Ramotswe. That was not because she believed he was really up there, but he was, in a sense. He was somewhere; she was sure of it. Whatever it was that had been within him, that part of us that we may find it hard to identify or describe—that bit would always be there, always. Late people, Mma Ramotswe said, are still with us. Of course they were—of course they were.

But you cannot think such things for long when you have to get to the shops before they close. Big thoughts like that should be kept for other occasions, when you do not have to buy the food for dinner and get back in time to make it before the family starts to complain that their evening meal is late. The people who thought about such weighty subjects, and who even wrote books about such things, did not have to make dinner—that was clear enough, she thought.

Once inside the building, she felt the relief of the cooled air on her skin. She suspected that there were people who visited the supermarket on particularly hot days not to buy anything, but simply to enjoy the air conditioning. She had seen some of them, standing near the refrigerated food section, pretending to take a great interest in the price labels displayed on the open cabinets, but actually taking the opportunity to make phone calls or chat to their friends while escaping the heat outside. Mma Makutsi had seen this too. She had recognised one of these people from her days at the Botswana Secretarial College, a woman who had been friendly with Violet Sephotho, and who had eventually been asked to leave the college after being caught cheating in the examinations. It had been no surprise to anybody when she had gone on to work for a lawyer who was widely regarded as unscrupulous, whom she subsequently married. Now here she was holding court in the refrigerated section of the supermarket, part of what Mma Makutsi described as the "cool set."

But when she entered the supermarket, Mma Ramotswe did not see this woman, nor any of the cool set, but Mma Makutsi herself, who was pushing a shopping cart through the vegetable section while at the same time consulting a shopping list. Mma Ramotswe saw her stop at the avocado pear section, lean forward and prod the displayed fruit with a forefinger.

Mma Ramotswe came up behind her. "Still unripe, I think, Mma."

Mma Makutsi spun round. "Oh, Mma Ramotswe, it's you." She pointed to the avocados. "Those are days off being ripe, Mma. If you bought those to put in a salad tonight, your teeth would break. They're rock hard."

"It is difficult for these supermarket people," said Mma Ramotswe. "If they put them out when they're already ripe, then a day or two later they're much too ripe. And then people will complain that they're too soft."

In Mma Makutsi's view, this was typical of Mma Ramotswe's willingness to look at things from the point of view of others. She herself was not so ready to find excuses for others, and never hesitated to let people know if some service they were providing was not up to scratch. On one occasion, a dress made for her by a local seamstress had gone back six times for various adjustments, until eventually the seamstress had taken to pretending to be out if she saw Mma Makutsi's car draw up outside. And then, on another, a painter who had been engaged to paint her kitchen—a man who regularly decorated Phuti Radiphuti's furniture store—became so fed up with being asked to attend to missed corners that he disappeared off the job altogether and refused ever again to work for the Double Comfort Furniture Store. Phuti had been tactful. "It's possible that you said something to offend him, Grace," he began, and then, seeing the reaction that this was provoking, he went on to say, "Of course, these people can be temperamental. I suppose that they're artists, in their way, and we all know that artists are difficult."

"He is not an artist," said Mma Makutsi. "He is a house painter. And he has left a big square of plaster under the basin unpainted. If painters do not think you will look somewhere, then they do not paint it. It is very bad."

Now, as they stood and looked at the offending avocados, Mma Ramotswe said, "Oh well, I might buy one or two of those. I am in no hurry to eat them. They can ripen in my kitchen."

Mma Makutsi consulted her list. "Cooking oil," she said. "I mustn't forget cooking oil, Mma Ramotswe."

"No, Mma, cooking oil is very important—"

Mma Makutsi cut her short. "Mr. J.L.B. Matekoni had a visitor this afternoon, Mma," she said. "It was while you were out at Mma Potokwane's place."

"Oh yes, Mma? Who was it?"

Mma Makutsi's face took on a pained expression. "He said that he was called Mr. Freddie Mogorosi. That's what he called himself."

Mma Ramotswe wondered why there should be any doubt about the name. Was his real name not Freddie Mogorosi? She waited for Mma Makutsi to continue.

"Mr. J.L.B. Matekoni brought him in for a cup of tea," Mma Makutsi went on. "They drank it outside."

"I see." This was no surprise: Mr. J.L.B. Matekoni often took his mug of tea outside to drink it under one of the acacia trees. He liked to watch the world from the shade of the large tree at the back of the garage, away from the noise and disturbance of the workshop.

Mma Makutsi hesitated. She never criticised Mr. J.L.B. Matekoni and was concerned that any comment she passed regarding Mr. Freddie Mogorosi might be taken as a rebuke to Mr. J.L.B. Matekoni—a suggestion, perhaps, that he was not sufficiently discerning in his choice of friends.

"Do you know this Mogorosi?" she asked Mma Ramotswe. "Have you ever heard of him before?"

Mma Ramotswe had not. "I knew some Mogorosis who lived down in Lobatse," she said. "There was a Thomas Mogorosi, who had a small printing business. He was married to a woman who used to work in the Ministry of Health. This woman had been a theatre nurse at the hospital before she went to work in the ministry offices. I never knew her, although I saw her husband many times. Of course there are other Mogorosis—many of them. It is a common name, as you know, Mma."

"I think I have heard Phuti talking about those Lobatse Mogorosis. I think this Mr. Freddie Mogorosi is a different sort of Mogorosi. I think . . ." Mma Makutsi's voice trailed off; it seemed to Mma Ramotswe that she was unsure whether she should continue.

Mma Ramotswe knew her colleague well enough to realise that this meant she had reservations. Whenever Mma Makutsi's voice disappeared like this, it was because something was worrying her.

"I think you may not like Mr. Freddie Mogorosi, Mma. Am I right about that?"

Mma Makutsi studied her fingernails. That was another sign, thought Mma Ramotswe.

"I never said that I didn't like him," sniffed Mma Makutsi.

Mma Ramotswe smiled. "But you didn't like him, did you, Mma?" And then, to soften any implication that there was an element of accusation in this, she added, "We can't like everybody, Mma Makutsi. There are some people who are just . . ." She searched for the right way of putting it. Every word that suggested itself seemed too strong: horrid, awful, dreadful, terrible . . . Very few people deserved these extreme descriptions, because most people, in spite of their manifest failings, had at least some good qualities. Take Violet Sephotho, for instance. Violet was far from perfect, but at least she—Mma Ramotswe stopped. She was trying to think of Violet's good qualities, but nothing was coming to her. Yet her initial point stood: every general observation had its lone exception somewhere.

Mma Ramotswe decided that sometimes the most charitable word was the best. "There are some people who are just very *trying*."

"Possibly," Mma Makutsi replied. "In fact, you could say that, Mma Ramotswe."

Mma Ramotswe nodded. "You know that I always trust your judgement, Mma. You know that, don't you?"

Mma Makutsi had been tense; now she seemed to relax. "Thank you, Mma." She lowered her voice, although there was nobody near them in the vegetable section. "There is something about him that

I just did not like," she said. "I'm not prejudiced, of course—I am a very fair person, I believe."

Mma Ramotswe was loyal. "Of course," she said.

"I found him a bit loud, Mma. Some people have loud voices. He is one. I am not saying it is his fault. I am not saying that."

Mma Ramotswe waited.

"It's just that I have been surprised," Mma Makutsi went on, "that we have had two questionable men come into the agency within a short time. There was Mr. Excellence Modise, and now there is this Mr. Freddie Mogorosi. This is very surprising, Mma. Why are there so many men like that coming to our door, I wonder." She paused. "But be that as it may, Mma, I sensed that this Mr. Freddie Mogorosi was not a person one would *trust*. He is not the sort of person one would choose to be with, if you see what I mean."

Mma Ramotswe frowned. "You mean you would not choose to be with him if you were . . . if you were a lady? Is it that sort of thing, Mma?"

They both knew what they were talking about. There were some men who made women feel uncomfortable because their manner was suggestive, or even leering. These were men who might make unwelcome advances, believing, as some of them did, that women found them irresistible. It was a sad category of men, made up of people who had never really been popular with women and who never would be. Yet such men had to be dealt with firmly, and told that they were not to make women feel uncomfortable through their talk and their posturing. In her professional life, Mma Ramotswe had occasionally had to deliver such a lecture to such a man, and on one occasion had even had to invoke the help of Mma Potokwane to get the message across. Mma Potokwane was a woman who knew how to handle men, and was always happy to come to the defence of any woman who was being pestered by a badly behaved one.

But it transpired that this was not the issue with Mr. Freddie Mogorosi. "I do not think that this Mogorosi is one of these ladies' men," said Mma Makutsi. "Men who are like that often dress in a particular way. They look at you from the side of their eyes. They stand too close to you—that sort of thing."

"And he was not like that?"

"No. He didn't get too close. And he didn't use any familiar language."

"So, what was it, Mma?"

Mma Makutsi hesitated. It was hard to find the words to express a feeling of disquiet, or a tingle at the back of the neck, but there was usually no mistaking it when you felt such things. And in this case, of course, there had been the warning that had come from her shoes. That had been unambiguous, but it was not the sort of thing you could talk openly about. If you said, "My shoes said to me . . ." then people would look at you and shake their heads; they would whisper among themselves; they would conclude that there was something wrong with you. And of course, there was no question of the shoes actually talking—not in reality, because shoes were inanimate objects, which suggested that any idea she had of the shoes talking was just that, and no more—an idea in her mind, an impression. And yet, and yet . . . she was not making anything up: she had heard what the shoes had said, and it accorded with her own impression of Mr. Freddie Mogorosi.

Mma Ramotswe was looking at her with that quizzical, reflective look that she employed when she was thinking hard about something. "Tell me, Mma Makutsi," she said at last, "you didn't get any advice from . . ." And at this point, she looked down at Mma Makutsi's shoes.

Mma Makutsi pursed her lips. "If my shoes had an opinion,

Mma," she said, "I think it would be exactly the same as mine—in this case at least."

Mma Ramotswe nodded. Nothing had been said, though, of the reason for Mr. Mogorosi's visit, and now she asked Mma Makutsi about that. Had Mr. Freddie Mogorosi brought a car in for repair? Mma Makutsi replied that she thought he had, but she was not certain. She had formed the opinion, though, that he and Mr. J.L.B. Matekoni were on friendly terms. "I could see that Mr. J.L.B. Matekoni did not share my misgivings about Mogorosi," she said. "He was smiling at him, Mma. I think that they were becoming big friends." She shook her head in disapproval, and then added, "Not that this is any of my business, Mma."

There was shopping to be done, and they said goodbye. Mma Ramotswe did not linger, and within twenty minutes she had bought all the groceries, paid for them, and was on her way home in her white van. It was almost dusk now, and the sky was copper-red over the Kalahari to the west. Each evening, she thought, we are reminded of how fortunate we are to live in this country, with all its displays of nature. We are reminded by these flaming sunsets, which make the sky red with fire, even if we sometimes do not even notice them. The familiar beauty of the world frequently goes unnoticed because we have other things to think about—and she was thinking now of Mma Makutsi's account of the visitor whom she had missed. If Mr. Freddie Mogorosi was as good a friend of Mr. J.L.B. Matekoni as Mma Makutsi seemed to suggest he was, then why had she never heard of him? There had to be a perfectly reasonable explanation, she told herself, because she and Mr. J.L.B. Matekoni had never kept any secrets from one another—as far as she knew, that is. There was no reason he would wish to conceal a friendship—once again, as far as she knew. That was how it should be between husband and wife, she felt: a man and a woman should endow each other with all their worldly goods and with all the secrets of their heart. That, she thought, lay at the heart of marriage—along with a willingness to do one's share of the washing-up, laughing at each other's jokes, and a resolution, on the husband's part, to clean the bath after each use. Those things might sound unimportant, but they were actually central to a good and lasting marriage. That, she told herself, had always been well known.

CHAPTER FIVE

THE WEAKER BRETHREN

MR. J.L.B. MATEKONI worked late at the garage that evening, with the result that by the time he arrived back home at Zebra Drive, Mma Ramotswe had already prepared their dinner. She had decided on sausages, pumpkin, and green beans—a meal that she knew he liked and that was easy enough to prepare. There were some evenings that seemed right for complex recipes, and others that were more suited to a simple dish of meat and vegetables, it all being a question of energy. This evening was one of the latter.

"That is a very good smell, Mma," he said as he came through the kitchen door. "I was hoping that tonight would be a night for sausages."

Mma Ramotswe smiled. "You have been working very hard, Rra. Sausages are very good for building up strength."

He went off to wash his hands. It was the lot of mechanics to have greasy hands, and giving them a good scrub at the end of the day was a familiar ritual. He had stressed to his apprentices the need to remove grease if one wanted to avoid problems with one's skin, but it had been an uphill battle—particularly with Charlie. He had known mechanics who had ended up with hands so cracked and rough that shaking hands with them was like grasping sandpaper—"You don't want to end up like that when you are older, Charlie," he said.

He could tell that Charlie was unmoved by the warning, as the young man simply shrugged and said, "*Ya, ya.*" That was typical of young people, thought Mr. J.L.B. Matekoni. They said *ya, ya* and then did nothing. They thought that the things that happened to older people would never happen to them—and yet they would. You could be saying *ya, ya* one moment and the next you were fifty and you had rough hands. Life had a way of happening rather quickly.

Mma Ramotswe put his dinner on the table in front of him. "I will say grace, Rra," she said.

She bowed her head. The house was quiet, as the children were away at a school function. It was just the two of them—Mma Ramotswe and Mr. J.L.B. Matekoni.

"We are grateful for the food that is on our table," she said. "There are many who do not have good food like this. We think of them, and hope that one day these brothers and sisters will have good things too."

Mr. J.L.B. Matekoni said, "Amen"—prematurely, as Mma Ramotswe had intended to add a few further observations, but now did not do so. She remembered Mma Makutsi, who had once explicitly qualified her wishes for the sustenance of others with the words "provided they are deserving of such benefits." That was not in the normal spirit of things, thought Mma Ramotswe, but she did not pursue the matter with Mma Makutsi, who occasionally said things that, on reflection, she admitted she did not mean. Mma Makutsi was not unkind, nor was she unsympathetic. At the same time, when it came to those whom Mma Ramotswe sometimes described as the "weaker brethren," she had been known to express the opinion that they would do well to pull their socks up. "We could all sit about and say how unfair the world is," she said, "but where does that get us, Mma? The answer, as often as not, is nowhere."

Mma Ramotswe acknowledged that there was some truth in that, but at the same time, she said, we had to remember that there were people who were doing their best, and still getting nowhere. That might not be their fault, she said, and if one could give them a hand up, then why not? Had not Mma Makutsi herself been helped by members of her family who had gone so far as to sell livestock in order to help her to get to the Botswana Secretarial College? "Not that I'm saying you've forgotten that, Mma Makutsi," said Mma Ramotswe. "It's just that sometimes we need to remind ourselves about how we got to where we've got. Just a suggestion, Mma."

Now, grace having been said, Mr. J.L.B. Matekoni was tackling his sausages and pumpkin with vigour.

"Mma Makutsi tells me," Mma Ramotswe began, "that you had a visitor today. She said that he came in for tea."

Mr. J.L.B. Matekoni had a mouth full of sausage, and so it took a few moments for him to reply. "Yes, Mma," he said. "Freddie Mogorosi called in. We drank a cup of tea together out under the tree—it was too hot inside, I thought."

"Yes," said Mma Ramotswe. "It was very hot, Rra."

"I don't think you've met him," continued Mr. J.L.B. Matekoni.

Mma Ramotswe was quick to say that she thought she had not. "I wondered if I had heard the name somewhere," she went on. "But I don't think I have."

"No," said Mr. J.L.B. Matekoni. "Perhaps not." He paused for a moment as he contemplated the remaining portion on his plate. Then he muttered, "It all goes so quickly."

Mma Ramotswe smiled. "Life? Or . . ."

"Sausages and pumpkin. Things that you particularly like to eat."

"Ah."

"Mind you," he said. "Life too."

She nodded her agreement. Mr. J.L.B. Matekoni occasionally commented on how mechanics could not be expected to have views on the more complex issues of life, but she felt, and had pointed this out to him, that he was being unduly modest in that regard. Mechanics were every bit as sensitive as other people—perhaps even more so. They *understood*, because they had to. They listened—to engines and to the people who relied on machines—which was every single one of us—and, at the end of the day, they coaxed the malfunctioning or inert back to life. That required a particular sort of feeling, one that mechanics, in her experience, often had. She would not hear a disparaging word about mechanics.

"You are right about life, Mr. J.L.B. Matekoni," she said. "When we are young, they say to us, 'It's going to go very quickly,' and we do not think that this can possibly be true. We think that this is just one of those things that adults say and that as children we know to be false. And then we reach our thirtieth birthday and we say, 'Well, maybe it is going a bit fast—not *very* fast, but certainly we can see that it is going.' And then other birthdays come along and maybe you are just a little bit slower getting up out of your chair than you used to be, and you think, well, perhaps. And then you look about you and you see that there are young people everywhere, and they do not seem to *notice* you, and that makes you think. And then, before you know it, you find yourself saying, 'It was different in the old days,' and you realise that the person you're talking to was only a child in those old days and doesn't remember them at all. And then you ask yourself what it was that they said about how time went quickly, and you remember how you did not think it true, but it is, of course, and you feel a bit sad, really, because none of us wants to say goodbye to the place we love, and the people too . . ."

It was a long speech, and she wondered at the end of it whether she should have said these things. Did we need to be reminded of the fact that one of these days it would be over, or should we just go about our daily business without thinking of that? She was not sure. You should not pretend that the world was different from the way it was, but did it help to think about these things—when you knew that thinking about them could not possibly change any of them?

She pondered this while her own sausages and pumpkin began to get cold on the plate before her. Then she noticed that Mr. J.L.B. Matekoni had eaten his last sausage and had almost finished his helping of pumpkin, and with that instinct that so many women have, that wonderful caring feeling for those whom they loved, she speared a sausage on her fork and passed it over to him. Then she followed this with the transfer of a spoonful of pumpkin.

He said, "Oh, Mma, you should not give me yours when I have been greedily eating all mine up."

"Hush," she said.

He did not protest further.

She asked him, "This Mogorosi, Rra: How did you get to know him?"

His answer was immediate, and simple: "Motor Trades Association."

"He's a member?"

Mr. J.L.B. Matekoni nodded. "He has that big franchise garage. You know the one. Out on the Molepolole Road. That place where they sell those expensive German cars. That place."

She had driven past the garage and its showroom many times. She called it Flash Motors, although that, of course, was not its real name. But it was flashy, whichever way you looked at it.

"I've met him at meetings sometimes," he continued. "Also, at big events. You know, sometimes his business has public days where they show a new model and they invite everybody along. I've been to one or two of those."

Her curiosity about Mr. Freddie Mogorosi was largely assuaged. He was simply another of Mr. J.L.B. Matekoni's motoring contacts. She came across these people from time to time—suppliers of spare parts, other mechanics, and so on, but found it difficult to remember exactly who was who.

"He brought his car in," said Mr. J.L.B. Matekoni. "It's one of their older models. He doesn't drive a new Mercedes. He prefers an older one. It's a good car. Those Germans make very good cars. Or, put it this way, there are German machines that make very good cars." He smiled. "There is a difference, you know. Now they have machines with long mechanical arms, and they cut the steel and put the car together. They are all robots. And the people sit in the office and drink tea and watch while the machines make the cars for them. That is the sort of world we're living in now, Mma Ramotswe."

Mma Ramotswe was thinking—not of those factories with their tireless machines, but of the practical issue of why Mr. Freddie Mogorosi, proprietor of one of the largest garages in Botswana, should bring his own car to Mr. J.L.B. Matekoni for attention. Surely his own garage, she thought, would have more than enough mechanics to attend to the boss's car. Of course, Mr. J.L.B. Matekoni had a considerable reputation as a mechanic—consulting him was perhaps rather like consulting an eminent surgeon—but it still seemed strange that Mr. Mogorosi should look outside his own enterprise when it would be so easy to have the car attended to on his own premises.

She put this to him now, and she could tell that the same thought had occurred to him.

"Yes," he said. "You are right, Mma. I was a bit surprised that he had brought the car to me for what was really a pretty straightforward service. All I had to do was to change the engine oil and put in a new air filter. There was nothing else to do."

She frowned. "Did he say anything about it? Did he tell you why he brought the car to you?"

Mr. J.L.B. Matekoni shook his head. "No," he said. "He did not. He just said: 'I've brought the car to you.' He also said that he would like to catch up. Those were his exact words. *I'd like to catch up.*" He shrugged. "I thought he was a bit lonely. He asked me whether I would go fishing with him. There is a boat that he sometimes uses on the dam. He said he could show me a place where there are some big fish to be caught."

"And you said you would go?"

Mr. J.L.B. Matekoni nodded. "I did. He wants to go on Saturday."

"I shall make you some sandwiches to take with you," Mma Ramotswe said.

"That would be good," said Mr. J.L.B. Matekoni, adding, "I don't think I shall catch anything. I never do."

She was surprised by this. He had never mentioned fishing. "You never do, Rra? I didn't know that you went fishing."

He looked sheepish. "Well, I don't—not actually. I was just saying that if I ever went fishing—which I don't, really—I wouldn't catch anything."

"You should not be defeatist, Rra. You have just as much chance as anybody else."

"I think he will catch them," said Mr. J.L.B. Matekoni. "He's good at most things."

"Really?"

"I mean, he's the type who *looks* as if he is good at everything."

She reflected on this in silence. She did not know Mr. Freddie Mogorosi, but she felt now that perhaps Mma Makutsi was right. Simply hearing about him set alarm bells ringing, even though she had never met him. It was very strange. But perhaps not: once you started to think that things were strange, they could seem even more puzzling, or even disturbing. And so it was best not to think that they were strange in the first place.

She did not think that Clovis Andersen had ever remarked on an issue like this in *The Principles of Private Detection*—but had he done so, it would have been interesting to see what he thought. On balance, she decided that Clovis Andersen would have found it strange, but perhaps not all that strange.

CHAPTER SIX

THE REAL BUSINESS. BIG TIME.

"NOW, CHARLIE," said Mma Ramotswe, as they inched along the quiet residential street off the airport road, "this is a very sensitive investigation. Anything involving matrimonial issues is very sensitive indeed. You know that, don't you?"

She glanced at the young man sitting in the passenger seat of her tiny white van. He had dressed smartly for the assignment—as she had asked him to do—and she noticed that he had shaved off the incipient moustache that Mma Makutsi had commented on a few days earlier. This pleased her, as Mma Ramotswe preferred men to be clean shaven. In fact, a clean-shaven man in a well-ironed white shirt and pressed blue trousers was, in her view, the very embodiment of masculine grooming. Charlie was wearing a white shirt—and it was well ironed and freshly laundered, she observed. That was a good start. His trousers, which were a shade of blue, had sharp creases running south from the waistband, which was another good sign. And his shoes, she was pleased to see, were well polished, even if the lace of one of them was frayed and did not look as if it would last much longer. That did not matter, though; the overall impression was one of neatness and concern over presentation, which was exactly the message that she would want any employee of the No. 1 Ladies' Detective Agency to give to the world. If the agency had a motto, she thought, it could be: *We care*. That was a reassuring thing to say to prospective clients, and the effect might even be improved by expanding it to read, *We care about your cares*. That was a nice sentiment. Everybody had at least some cares in this life, and it was always reassuring to know that there were people who were prepared to help you to shoulder whatever burden Fate had imposed. That was the point—the central pillar of the old Botswana morality: *look after one another*. That was it, in a nutshell, and you hardly needed to add anything to that, other than, perhaps, tagging on: *and be kind*.

Charlie answered her question: "Yes, Mma, I know that. Marriage . . . ow! Don't go there, I always say."

Mma Ramotswe frowned. "But you yourself are married, Charlie. Are you suggesting it's not a good idea? Is that what you're saying?"

"Oh, no, Mma—I'm not saying that people shouldn't get married. All I'm saying is that other people's marriages are private. That's where you shouldn't go."

Mma Ramotswe agreed. "That's true in general, Charlie. You should always leave friends to sort out their own matrimonial issues. But some people need the help of somebody else because they need to find something out. That is what we're doing here. We're acting for Mr. Excellence Modise. He is the client, you see."

Charlie understood. "Oh, I know all that, Mma. We have his authority. He has given us his . . . his . . ." He searched for the word, and eventually it came to him. "His consent."

"Precisely," said Mma Ramotswe. "And that is why we are looking for his house."

She peered out of the van window. Most of the houses had their plot numbers displayed on their gates but some of these had fallen off, or, having been allowed to fade, had become illegible. It was the sun that did that—the unrelenting sun could draw the colour out of paint and leave only ghost tracings behind. In the dry season, the sun could blanch an entire landscape, and sometimes did, until the rains came and brought colour back to the world.

Mma Ramotswe had been driving slowly; now she slowed the van almost to a walking pace. Excellence Modise had described the house to her. He had mentioned two large jacaranda trees in the front garden and a pair of white gates at the head of the drive. When she saw both of these features, she said to Charlie, "Look, we are there. See? Now we need to find somewhere to park. Somewhere not too close, but where we'll be able to watch."

They found such a spot, near enough to the Modise property but far enough away for them to watch discreetly. A large acacia tree, gnarled in the trunk but generous in its canopy, would provide the shade necessary for their vigil.

With the engine switched off, they heard the sound of cicadas, shrill in the warm air of the morning. Charlie cleared his throat. He shifted in his seat. "Will we have to sit here for hours, Mma? Hours and hours?"

Mma Ramotswe smiled. She reminded herself that Charlie belonged to the *now* generation, to whom everything had to happen in the present, immediately. "I take it that you don't want to do that, Charlie?"

"Oh, I don't mind, Mma. It's just a bit boring, that's all."

Mma Ramotswe was sympathetic. She remembered being bored when she was his age. She remembered waiting for things to occur, and often they did not. It was harder when you were at Charlie's stage in life, when excitement was what you wanted.

"We might not have to wait all that long, Charlie," she said. "Mr. Modise said that he thinks his wife goes out round about the middle of the morning." She glanced at her watch. "That should be soon enough."

"Why doesn't he follow her himself?" asked Charlie. There was a note of peevishness in his voice, and Mma Ramotswe picked this up. She wanted to say to him, "But this is work, Charlie—and work often consists of doing things that other people do not want to do—or cannot do themselves." She did not say this, though. Charlie would learn—eventually; although if he was keen to be promoted from his current post—junior assistant detective, according to Mma Makutsi—he would have to work on his reasoning powers. He was not an unintelligent young man, but he needed to learn how to think logically and not to ask questions that had only too obvious answers.

"Mr. Modise cannot follow his wife," she explained, "because she would wonder what he was doing, driving after her in his pest control van. And if she was going somewhere that she didn't want anybody to know about, would she go there with her husband trailing behind her? I don't think so, Charlie."

"No," said Charlie. "I suppose not."

He started to whistle. It was a tune that Mma Ramotswe did not recognise, but she hardly expected that she would. She knew the sort of music that Charlie and Fanwell liked, as it drifted in from the garage when they were working there. This sometimes resulted in Mma Makutsi's storming out and complaining that it was impossible to do anything with a constant din coming from next door. "I cannot concentrate if there is that rubbish music playing all the time," she said. "*Boom, boom, boom*. That is all it is. *Boom, boom, boom*."

Now, as they sat in the van under the shade of the acacia tree, Mma Ramotswe said to Charlie, "What is that tune you're whistling, Charlie? I don't mind it—you can whistle if you want, but I just want to know what it's called."

He seemed surprised. "Everybody knows that tune, Mma. *Boom, boom, boom.* They play it all the time on the radio. It's big."

"I'm sure it is, Charlie," she said. "But I don't know it."

"It's called 'I've Got Big Love for You.' It's about a boy who—"

"Is in love with a girl?"

Charlie looked impressed. "How did you know that, Mma?"

Mma Ramotswe was modest. "I worked it out from the title, Charlie."

"I don't know all the words," said Charlie. "But he says to this girl that he's been watching her and he thinks they should go out. She says that she doesn't want to go out because it's too cold. So, he says she will be warm in his arms. Those are the words, Mma. It is very clever."

She suppressed a smile. There were so many songs about love and so few about . . . She thought of the things that songwriters might celebrate. Cooking? Watching cattle move through the trees in search of better grazing? The wind that sometimes sprang from the Kalahari and touched your skin with its dry fingers? Sitting in a van under a tree and waiting for a woman to come out of a house and go off to meet a lover? That brought one back to men and women, so that would just be another love song . . .

And there she was. She was coming out of the house and saying something to a man who had been raking a flower bed in the garden. The Modise gardener, of course, who was now scratching his head and pointing towards the far side of the garden, where there were two or three dispirited-looking paw-paw trees.

She nudged Charlie, who stopped whistling and whispered, "That's her, Mma. That's her. And she's talking to a man, Mma. You see that? That could be the man who—"

She cut him short. "That's the gardener, Charlie. He has a rake in his hand, and so we think: *gardener*. That's the conclusion we draw. Lovers do not hold rakes, you see."

Charlie was unabashed. "Possibly, Mma."

"Definitely," she said.

The woman moved away, and the man continued to rake the flower bed.

"Now she's getting into her car, you see," said Mma Ramotswe. "We'll just wait here, and then we'll follow her."

"That's right," said Charlie. "We'll follow her, Mma. Then we'll see where she's going. She'll lead us to this man she's seeing."

"Possibly," said Mma Ramotswe.

An apposite dictum from *The Principles of Private Detection* came to her. *Do not imagine*, wrote Clovis Andersen, *that people will do what you think they will do. That may lead you to misinterpret their actions. Be prepared for surprises.*

She summarised this for Charlie. "Don't assume anything, Charlie. Always wait and see."

"So, she could just be going shopping?" Charlie suggested.

"That's right. We'll see in due course."

Charlie nodded. "This is very exciting, Mma Ramotswe," he said. "This is the real business. Big time."

She felt she had to keep his excitement in check. "You could say that, Charlie. But don't get ahead of yourself. Sometimes there's not much to see." She paused. "Sometimes, when we expect a lot to happen, it doesn't. That is well known, I think."

BUT THAT MORNING, rather a lot happened, most of it unexpected. And they did not have long to wait; in fact, no sooner had Mma Modise negotiated her way out of the driveway in a large brown car, than

Mma Ramotswe's mission came unstuck. Without giving any notice, the normally obedient van chose this moment to refuse to start.

As the starter motor whined unproductively, Charlie gave a set of instructions. "Put your foot on the accelerator, Mma. Give her more fuel. Not too much, Mma. You don't want to flood the engine. Turn off the ignition and start again. No, don't use all the battery power—not too much. Turn off again."

After a couple of minutes, the remaining power in the battery gave out.

"That's the trouble, Mma," said Charlie. "Your battery levels were low."

Outside the van, the shriek of the cicadas seemed to become louder.

"What now?" asked Mma Ramotswe, adding, "This is very bad timing, Charlie."

"That is always when cars won't start," said Charlie. "They always choose the wrong moment."

"Do we walk?" asked Mma Ramotswe.

"We cannot follow a car on foot," said Charlie. "That wouldn't work, Mma."

"I know that, Charlie. I was suggesting that we might have to walk back into town."

Charlie hesitated. Then he opened the passenger door and got out. Through the window he informed Mma Ramotswe that they could try to push-start the van. "I'll push, Mma. You put us in gear, but keep your foot on the clutch. Then, after we get going, you take your foot off the clutch, and we start."

Mma Ramotswe nodded. She had done this before, when her battery had run down at a remote cattle post and she had been far from help. It had worked, but only after a team of three helpful and well-built men had pushed the van over several hundred yards. Would Charlie have the staying power to do that?

He took up his position at the rear of the van and shouted for her to engage the clutch. There was a slight incline where they had parked, and it did not take much effort on his part to get the van moving. And then, when Mma Ramotswe removed her foot from the clutch pedal, the engine jerked into life.

Unfortunately, Mma Ramotswe was unprepared for the sudden burst of power, and found herself wrestling with the steering wheel as the van shot off across the road. She might narrowly have avoided disaster were it not for the fact that the sleeve of her blouse caught on the gear lever. Momentarily out of control, the van crossed the road, heading for the gates of the Modise house. By the time Mma Ramotswe managed to engage the clutch and apply the brake, it was too late. With a shuddering crunch, the van hit one of the gate posts, knocking it several degrees off true.

Within moments, Charlie was beside her open window, gasping. "Are you all right, Mma?"

She nodded. "I have bumped into that gate post," she said.

"I see that, Mma," said Charlie. "And your van has a dent now." He stepped back to inspect the damage. "Not a bad one, though, and I can fix it for you. I can get a hammer and knock it back into shape. It is nothing, Mma."

"And the gate?"

Charlie strode over to the gate post and pulled it back into position. "There," he said. "Nobody will notice that."

"Except me," said a voice behind him.

It was the gardener.

Charlie turned round to address him. "I am sorry, Rra," he said. "This was an accident." He gestured towards Mma Ramotswe, still in the van. "This poor lady lost control of her van. We were push-starting it, you see."

The gardener examined the post. "There is no damage," he said. Then he added, "A pity."

Charlie looked puzzled.

The gardener smiled. "These people—" He inclined his head back towards the house. "These people are no good, Rra. Or rather, *she's* no good. He's not so bad, but she's . . ." He shook his head. "I wouldn't care at all if you had knocked the gate off altogether. That will teach her, I'd say."

Charlie's astonishment was obvious. "I—" he began, but it was clear that he had no idea how to finish.

The gardener wiped his brow. "I'm sorry if I sound rude, Rra. It's just that I have never liked this Mr. Excellence man—the man who lives here. Excellence in what? I ask. Being pleased with himself, if you ask me. He gets top marks for that."

Mma Ramotswe had been following this conversation. Now she emerged from the car and introduced herself to the gardener. "I am very sorry about the gate," she said. "The van ran away with itself."

The gardener assured her that it did not matter at all.

"But I am sorry to hear, Rra," Mma Ramotswe went on, "that you have to work for somebody you don't like. That can't be easy."

The gardener sighed. "There are not enough jobs to go round, Mma. You have to take what you can get."

Mma Ramotswe nodded. "But you say that he's not too bad?"

"That's right," said the gardener. "I don't see how he puts up with her. Perhaps there are not enough wives to go round."

Mma Ramotswe laughed. "Was that her driving out of the gate just then?" she asked. She made the question sound as casual as she could.

"It was," came the reply.

"Going shopping, I suppose," said Mma Ramotswe. "These ladies with a lot of money. They have so much shopping to do, don't they?"

The gardener hesitated. "Not shopping, I think, Mma. She goes to that garden place. You know the one? It is called Sanitas. You will know it, Mma. They have a restaurant under the trees. She sits there and eats pizza. I have seen her. I have gone there with my other employer—I look after three gardens altogether, you see. I have been there to get plants for one of the other gardens. She is always there, I think."

Mma Ramotswe grinned. "She must be a hungry lady—eating pizza all day."

"And talking with her friends," added the gardener. "I have seen her. Not only talking with other ladies but with men, Mma. I have gone past that place when she is there. I have seen her."

Mma Ramotswe glanced at Charlie. He inclined his head slightly. This had been a lesson for him; he had been paying attention and was impressed. This was how to get information. Mma Ramotswe made it seem so easy.

"I think we mustn't take up your time, Rra," said Mma Ramotswe.

"I don't mind, Mma."

She reached out to touch his forearm. "I hope that things go better for you, Rra. I hope that you find a job where you are a bit happier."

The gardener looked at her with gratitude. "You are very kind, Mma. And yes, I am planning something. I have applied for a job at one of the hotels. They have a garden that is a big mess and they need somebody to sort it out for them." He paused. "Why do people let their gardens get out of control, Mma? That is what I can't understand."

"People can be foolish," said Mma Ramotswe. "Not all of them, but some can. And then they need people like you to come and sort everything out."

The compliment was well received. Once again, he said, "You are very kind, Mma."

Mma Ramotswe had inadvertently switched off the engine. A second push-start was now needed, this time powered by Charlie and the gardener. It worked just as well, and they were soon driving down the road towards the turn-off that would lead them eventually to the Sanitas garden.

Charlie looked with admiration at Mma Ramotswe. "You made that man feel much better, Mma. Did you see him at the end? When you told him that we needed men like him to sort things out, he was all puffed up—he was that pleased."

"I didn't just say it, Charlie, I meant it."

"Well, he was very pleased, I think."

"It is easy to make people feel better, Charlie. Try to remember that. Tell them that they are doing a good job, and you can see the result." She gave him a sideways glance. "You, for instance—you're doing a good job, Charlie."

"Oh, Mma . . ."

"But always remember that there is room for improvement. That applies to all of us, by the way."

"*Ya, ya,*" said Charlie.

CHAPTER SEVEN

―――――――

ALL MEN SEEM HANDSOME

THEY ARRIVED at the Sanitas Tea Garden fifteen minutes later. The car park was almost full, but Mma Ramotswe found a spot near the gate and took this before anybody else could claim it. As she emerged from the van, she cast her eye around the rows of vehicles already there. It was a Saturday morning, and the garden centre was busy with people stocking up on shrubs and other plants for the impending rainy season. Mma Ramotswe herself had been there only a week or two before, buying bean plants and onion bulbs for her vegetable garden. It was a sociable place, and after she had made her purchase, she spent rather longer than she had planned over tea with friends who had also been stocking up on their garden supplies.

"Over there, Mma," whispered Charlie, pointing to the far end of the car park.

She looked over in the direction in which he pointed. Her gaze must have passed over it before, but now she saw it: the large brown car in which Mma Modise had left the house on the other side of town. She felt a certain satisfaction that her brief conversation with the gardener had saved them the bother of tailing Mma Modise.

Although she was confident that she knew how to follow somebody without being spotted, there was always a chance that the person being followed would look in the mirror and wonder why her car seemed so tenacious.

"Now remember, Charlie," she warned, as they began to make their way through the entrance of the garden centre, "try not to stare. Look at the plants—not at the people. Pretend to be interested in compost and seedlings and so on."

Charlie assured her that merging with his surroundings was something at which he was quite adept. "They never see me, Mma," he said. "Mr. Invisible—that's who I am."

She smiled. "And me, Charlie? Am I Mrs. Inconspicuous?"

Charlie grinned. "You're a bit too traditionally built, Mma, to be inconspicuous. No offence—it's just that . . . well, you aren't, I think."

She gave him a look of mock reproach, and he grinned back unapologetically. Then, appearing to all intents and purposes like a woman accompanied by a nephew, perhaps, looking for garden plants, they entered the large, shade-netted shopping area. It was cool, and there was the sound of water playing down several demonstration fountains; the smell of tree bark and fruitfulness.

"It smells *green* in here," muttered Charlie, appreciatively.

Mma Ramotswe pointed to an area on the far side of the enclosure. This was shaded by a canopy of foliage, of trees, of creepers, of vines, and underneath were tables and chairs. A couple of waitresses, wearing green tunics, moved between the tables, carrying laden trays. "Over there, Charlie. I can see where we need to go."

She had only had a brief glimpse of Mma Modise when she had seen her talking to the gardener, but she was able to recognise the bright floral dress she had been wearing. Now, by fortunate chance, the table next to the one at which Mma Modise was sitting was available, and she led Charlie to it. As she sat down, she made an effort not to look in Mma Modise's direction. Charlie took his cue from her, although she noticed that he sneaked several surreptitious glances at the neighbouring table.

Mma Modise was alone. She had opened a gardening magazine and was paging through it, sipping at the tea that had already been served. Suddenly alerted to something, she slipped the magazine into her bag and made an effort to compose herself.

He came up to the table, walking with the confidence of one whose arrival is both anticipated and welcomed. He was a tall man, dressed in an open-necked shirt and checked slacks. As he approached Mma Modise's table, he took off a pair of expensive-looking sunglasses. Then, leaning forward, he planted a kiss on her brow.

Charlie caught Mma Ramotswe's eye. "You see that," he whispered.

The man sat down and he and Mma Modise immediately engaged in conversation. She had something to tell him, it seemed, and she spoke with a degree of animation. In the hubbub of the outdoor tea room, with birds adding their bit to the general conversation, it was impossible for Mma Ramotswe and Charlie to make out what was being said, although the occasional word rose above the background noise—*impossible . . . Lobatse . . . easy enough . . . a bit more money . . . he said no, but . . .* It could have been a conversation about anything, as much a casual catching-up between friends as an exchange between lovers.

Yet there was no doubt in Mma Ramotswe's mind that this was a clandestine assignation, even if it was slightly surprising that it should be as public as this. In the old days, of course, nobody could go anywhere in Gaborone without being noticed, and meeting a lover in the Sanitas Tea Garden would have amounted to shouting the affair from the rooftops. It was different now, she realised, as there were more people, and when there were more people, there were always more strangers.

"What are we going to do, Mma?" whispered Charlie.

Mma Ramotswe leaned towards him and said out of the corner of her mouth, "Don't whisper too much. We must not look suspicious."

Charlie bit his lip. "Sorry, Mma." He cleared his throat. "It's still hot. I hope there'll be rain soon."

"Rain," said Mma Ramotswe. "It can't come too soon, Charlie."

"If there is rain, then there will be good crops," Charlie continued, now speaking at normal volume. "There will be a very big harvest."

Mma Ramotswe considered this gravely. "That is probably true, Charlie," she pronounced. "Crops do not like a drought, you know."

"And the dam will fill up again," said Charlie. "It is good when the dam is full of water."

"That is also true, I think," said Mma Ramotswe.

They noticed that there was silence from the next-door table. Mma Ramotswe noticed that Mma Modise had glanced in their direction, as had her companion. Had they overheard this conversation about rain? Was there something they might like to add to it? People in Botswana never tired of talking about rain—a common feature of conversations in a dry country.

Mma Modise stood up, followed by her companion. He reached out and brushed a fly from her shoulder. It was an intimate gesture, and for Mma Ramotswe it was further confirmation of what she had assumed. Then the two of them began to make their way towards the car park beyond the trees. Mma Ramotswe and Charlie remained where they were, although they did not persist with their attempt at casual conversation. Eventually Charlie said, "They have gone, Mma. I think we're safe now."

They got up from their table. On the way out, stopping at the cash desk where people paid for their gardening purchases, she greeted the attendant, a middle-aged woman in green overalls.

"Tell me, Mma," she said. "That couple who have just left. She was wearing that very pretty flower-dress—you probably saw her. He was a very handsome man."

The woman smiled. "All men seem handsome to me, Mma—at my age."

Mma Ramotswe laughed. "They never notice, though—do they?"

"Well," sighed the woman. "Perhaps it is better that way."

Mma Ramotswe waited. Then she asked, "So, do you know who they are, Mma? I thought I recognised them, but I can't be sure."

The woman looked out in the direction of the car park. "They are very fond of one another," she said.

Charlie's eyes widened.

"That's nice," said Mma Ramotswe.

"They're here a lot," said the woman. "Two or three times a week."

Mma Ramotswe raised an eyebrow. "Do you remember their names, Mma?"

The woman frowned. "She's called Aleseng."

Mma Ramotswe waited a few moments before asking, "And his name, Mma?"

"He's Bakang, I think. But I'm not sure. I thought I heard him being called something different."

"And his surname, Mma? Do you know that?"

The woman smiled. "The same as hers, I think. Thato." She looked bemused—as if she might be wondering why anybody should ask so obvious a question.

Mma Ramotswe hesitated. "But they aren't married, are they, Mma?"

The woman laughed. "Of course not. She's his sister."

This information was received in silence.

"Are you sure?" asked Mma Ramotswe.

The woman explained that they had once asked her to take a photograph of themselves at the table. "She introduced him as her brother," she said. "And I could see the resemblance." She paused. "I have remembered his family name. It *is* Thato, because I knew a Thato once who was a nurse at the clinic near us. She was a cousin, I think. But she is no longer Thato because she married a man called Modise—if I remember correctly. He has that pest control business—you may know it."

"Oh."

The woman continued, "And one of the cooks in the kitchen knows them. He said they were brother and sister. He was at school with them here in Gaborone."

It took some effort on Mma Ramotswe's part to conceal her surprise. *Don't be surprised by anything,* wrote Clovis Andersen. *The most unlikely thing is often the most likely. Remember that.* She did remember it, even if she thought there was something about the statement that, unusually for anything said by Clovis Andersen, did not seem to make a great deal of sense.

The woman behind the desk became distracted. Another customer had arrived at the till with goods to be paid for. "I'm sorry, Mma," she said, "but I must attend to this other lady."

Mma Ramotswe thanked her and accompanied Charlie into the car park.

"So, Mma," said Charlie, "that was a big waste of time, wasn't it?"

She was patient, and tried to explain. "Nothing is wasted in our work, Charlie," she said. "If you go up a blind alley, that is not a waste of time because you have discovered something—that there is no point in going that way. You learn from everything, you see—even the things that take you nowhere."

Charlie looked thoughtful. "So she goes out three times a week to meet up with her brother. I wonder why?"

Mma Ramotswe took a moment or two to consider her reply. Why would anybody do that? Family affection? Yes, possibly—but that often? Loneliness, perhaps? That was more likely, she thought. And relations between brothers and sisters could sometimes be very close, in some cases leading to people living under the same roof for much of their lives. Not everybody found marriage partners, and for some brothers and sisters, living together, or just seeing a great deal of one another, might make perfect sense. Why be lonely if you had family with whom you could share your life?

She turned to Charlie. "We get used to seeing the same people regularly, Charlie. Two or three times a week is not too much, I would say. We love to talk about what's going on. Those two had a lot to discuss, I think." She paused. She remembered what Excellence Modise had said about his wife—that she did not like him. If that was the case, then it was easy to see how she might just like to meet up with her brother and chat for a while—as a means of getting away from a domestic life in which she was unhappy. We all needed a friend with whom to take refuge—and for Mma Modise that appeared to be her brother.

They reached the van. Charlie was quiet, as if he was still pondering what they had just discovered. He looked disappointed, and Mma Ramotswe decided that he must have been hoping for a quick solution. But real life was rarely as simple as we would like it to be. The truth, which was something we sometimes uncovered and sometimes did not, was not always as easily established as all that. If you were watching somebody, it might take days, even months, before they revealed themselves. It was a long process, and patience was required. Charlie was young—and the young were sometimes impatient when it came to patience.

"What now?" asked Charlie as they got into the van.

"I try to start the engine," said Mma Ramotswe. "I hope that the battery is in a better mood."

Charlie corrected her. "It is not a question of mood, Mma Ramotswe," he said. "There's an alternator, see, in the engine. When the engine runs, the alternator creates a current that goes into the battery and recharges it. That is how it works."

She turned the key in the ignition, and the engine coughed into life.

"Bang!" said Charlie with satisfaction. "There is charge in the battery now. I can check it for you later, though, in case it is just too old. Batteries don't last forever, Mma. You have to replace them every five years—at least. Always replace your battery before it gets too old and tired, Mma." He paused. "How old is your battery, Mma?"

Mma Ramotswe shrugged. "I have never replaced it, as far as I know."

Charlie spoke accusingly. "But what about the boss? Surely, he's replaced it. He wouldn't let you drive around on a rubbish battery."

"Perhaps," said Mma Ramotswe vaguely. She did not like all this talk of batteries—not while she was about to drive off. Providence should not be tempted, she felt.

They drove off, heading back to the office on the Tlokweng Road. It had not been a successful morning, and Mma Ramotswe was wondering how she should take this particular investigation to its next stage. She could try following Mma Modise once more, but that might take her straight back to the Sanitas Tea Garden, and a repeat of today's experience. Or she could talk to the gardener again, and see if he had any further information to impart. That was a possibility, but she would have to think about it before she reached any decision.

Then Charlie said, "That car is behind us, Mma."

She did not take her eyes off the road. The traffic was building up, and other drivers could be unpredictable. "What car?" she asked.

"That woman's car, Mma. The one we saw."

Mma Ramotswe glanced in her rear-view mirror. Charlie was right. The large brown car was not far behind them, and Mma Ramotswe could even make out the figure of Mma Modise at the wheel. This was rather puzzling; she thought that the other woman had left before them, but she must have taken her time to get out of the car park.

Mma Ramotswe slowed down. The large brown car followed suit. She speeded up, with the same result.

"She's following us, Mma," said Charlie.

Mma Ramotswe frowned. "It may just be a coincidence, Charlie. Just because a car is behind you, it doesn't mean it's following you."

"Then why does it slow down, Mma, when we slow down? Is that coincidence as well? I may not be Mr. Encyclopedia BA, but I think that if a car behind you slows down when you slow down, then there's a good chance it's following you."

Mma Ramotswe looked in the mirror again, and then made up her mind. They were approaching a junction, and shortly before they reached it, she suddenly slowed down and swung the van off the road. She left the manoeuvre to the last minute, and the tiny white van almost strayed off its new course before she corrected it. Immediately after turning, she looked behind her, and saw the other car had turned too.

Mma Ramotswe sighed. "I think I am going to ignore her, Charlie. It could still be a coincidence. There will be many people who will turn off here. It doesn't mean they're following somebody."

Charlie looked doubtful. "Not very likely, Mma," he said. "But you're the one in charge. I am just the junior person here. I am not the one who knows about these things."

IN THE TIME OF FIVE PUMPKINS

THEY ARRIVED BACK AT the office of the No. 1 Ladies' Detective Agency. As Mma Ramotswe nosed the van into its accustomed parking place under its tree, she saw that Mma Modise's car had stopped further down the road, under a tree of its own. There was now no doubt in her mind that they had been followed, and when Charlie pointed the car out to her, she accepted that he had been right all along. He said, "Isn't it a bit unusual to go off and follow somebody and then be followed yourself? Has that ever happened to you before, Mma Ramotswe?"

"It is very unusual, Charlie. You are quite right."

He scratched his head. "So, what should we do, Mma? Should we just ignore her?"

Mma Ramotswe was undecided. "I'm not sure, Charlie. Perhaps we should think about it over a cup of tea."

Tea, of course, was always the solution to a difficult issue. Red bush tea, which was Mma Ramotswe's favourite, was particularly suited for that, as she found that not only did it clear the mind, but it seemed also to raise the spirits. It was hard to feel defeated by the world if you had a cup of red bush tea in your hand. It was possible, of course, but hard.

They went inside, where Charlie sat in Mma Makutsi's chair, as she was out of the office that day. "This is a very comfortable chair," he said. "I've noticed that other people's chairs are always more comfortable than your own—if you have a chair, of course." He looked across the room at Mma Ramotswe and added, "Which some of us do not."

Mma Ramotswe took a sip of her tea. "Interesting," she said. She was not paying particular attention to what Charlie was saying, but her mind was active. And now she reached her decision.

"Charlie," she said. "I would like you to step outside and speak to

Mma Modise. Invite her in for a cup of tea. Tell her that I do not like the thought of her sitting out there in the heat."

Charlie looked astonished. "But, Mma, she's been following us . . ."

"And we've been following her," Mma Ramotswe countered. "In such circumstances, I think the least we can do is offer her tea. Following people can be thirsty work."

CHAPTER EIGHT

I AM SO FORTUNATE

MA MODISE did not conceal her curiosity as she came through the door of the No. 1 Ladies' Detective Agency.

"So, this is what goes on in here," she said. "I have often driven past this place and wondered what goes on inside. I thought, That's a very small building for a business like this."

Mma Ramotswe smiled. "We don't need a big office, Mma," she said. "A lot of our work is done outside."

Mma Modise appeared to consider this. She nodded. "I can understand that. You're out following people, I suppose—just as—" She paused for effect. "Just as you've been following me."

Charlie looked away. It was a potentially embarrassing moment, but Mma Ramotswe was unfazed.

"Oh, I see," she said. She could hardly deny it, but that did not mean that she had to make any admissions. To say, "Oh, I see," was gloriously non-committal.

But if Mma Ramotswe was unforthcoming, Mma Modise was prepared to go further.

"I saw you parked outside my house, Mma," she said. "You were under a tree, not far along the road. I saw you sitting there with this young man here. You were both looking at my house. I have binoculars, you see. I was at my window, looking out with my binoculars. I thought: What is that lady doing there, watching me?"

Mma Ramotswe lowered her eyes. This was humiliating, and it made her feel as if she were a voyeur exposed—one of those people who love to look through other people's windows. There were various reasons why people did this: in some cases, it was simple curiosity about how others lived; in others, it was envy of the possessions and position of those doing better than themselves; or it could, of course, be much more sinister.

"And then," continued Mma Modise, "you turned up at the tea garden. That proved that I was not wrong—you were following me. You came and sat at the table next to mine. I thought: this lady is following me to find out something. And you talked about the rain because you didn't want to look as if you were watching me. You looked everywhere but at my table. That's unnatural, Mma—people always look at the table next to them. That would have been far less suspicious."

When she had finished this denunciation, Mma Modise gave Mma Ramotswe a look that was a clear challenge to her to deny what had been said. But Mma Ramotswe could not do that, because what had been said was entirely reasonable.

"So, what I'd like to know, Mma," Mma Modise went on, "is why? And you know what? I think I know the answer. I think I know who sent you to follow me. There can only be one person who would do that. My husband. It is my husband's doing, isn't it, Mma?"

Mma Ramotswe folded her hands. This gave rise to another difficult question: she liked to be truthful, but serious consequences could flow from telling a woman that her husband had arranged for her to be followed. Such information was hardly likely to promote matrimonial concord, although she suspected that in the case of the Modise marriage there was not much of that. More importantly, perhaps, was the entirely reasonable expectation of Mr. Excellence Modise that his wife would not be informed of his consultation with the No. 1 Ladies' Detective Agency. It was hard to argue with that.

Yet she did not like to lie, and so she said nothing.

Mma Modise raised a finger. "You don't need to answer, Mma. I know it's him."

"I'm sorry, Mma," began Mma Ramotswe. "But—"

Mma Modise cut her short. "It's very sad, Mma. I've done my best, you know. I've tried and tried to make our marriage work, but whatever I do never seems to be enough. He just doesn't like me, it seems. It's not my fault, Mma—it really isn't."

Mma Ramotswe's dismay showed. "Oh, Mma, this is awful."

"Yes," continued Mma Modise. "And there's another thing. He's started to have an affair."

Mma Ramotswe waited for her to elaborate. These matters could become complicated—*very* complicated in this case.

"That is why I was pleased when I realised that it was you following me. You see, I would like to engage you to find out what my husband is doing. It's not that this will have an effect on how our property is split up if we divorce. These days, they don't look at who caused the marriage to come to an end. But . . ."

Mma Ramotswe guessed what the concern would be. "You don't want people talking?"

"Exactly, Mma. I don't want people to go round saying it was my fault. That can be a big problem back in the village—not so much here, but in the village, tongues wag and you can easily be frozen out."

Mma Ramotswe drew in her breath. "But why would he accuse you of having an affair when that's what he's up to himself, Mma?"

"For the same reason," replied Mma Modise. "If he can show that I have gone off with somebody, then all the fingers will point at me. All the elders, all the aunties, everybody at the *kgotla*—they will all say that I am a fast lady who has let her husband down. That is what these people say, Mma. And before you know it, you have no reputation. None."

Mma Ramotswe thought about this: she could see that it made sense. She felt a certain distaste, though: Where was decency in all this? If people could not get on and had to go their separate ways, why could they not do it courteously and fairly? Because they were human—that was probably the answer to that. We all had human failings that we somehow had to overcome in our dealings with others. It was the only way, if life were to be anything but a battle for advantage.

She saw that Mma Modise was looking at her expectantly. "So, Mma, will you do this thing for me? I can pay you the normal rate. There is no problem with money."

Mma Ramotswe winced. This was not easy. "Tell me, Mma Modise," she said, "do you have grounds to suspect your husband of having an affair?"

The reply came quickly. "Very strong grounds, Mma Ramotswe. I am one hundred per cent sure."

"How?" asked Mma Ramotswe.

Mma Modise's expression became one of distaste. "I found something, Mma. I found an earring in the bathroom. I had been away for a few days, visiting my sister up in Maun. When I came back, I found the earring. There had been goings-on in my absence."

She watched for Mma Ramotswe's reaction to this.

"An earring?"

"Yes. A large earring. It was on the side of the basin. I still have it, and I could even show it to you. It has a bit of agate in the middle—that stripey agate they get up at Bobonong. And round the edge it's gold, but not real gold." She paused. "I know that some men have ear-piercings these days, Mma, but my husband is not one of those. He is the sort of man who would never wear jewellery. He is very old-fashioned. And I must say I agree with him, Mma—on that subject at least. Men should leave the wearing of jewellery to women, I think."

Mma Ramotswe was non-committal. "There are different views on that issue, Mma."

Charlie now intervened. "Earrings look cool on some men," he said. "If the man is cool to begin with, then earrings make him look even cooler. But if he isn't cool, if he's somebody like Mr. J.L.B. Matekoni—no offence, Mma Ramotswe—then it's best for him not to wear an earring."

The two women turned to look at him. Mma Modise looked doubtful; Mma Ramotswe was disapproving. This conversation could easily be sidetracked—and who was Charlie to describe Mr. J.L.B. Matekoni as not being cool? He did not *want* to be cool, of course, but that was another matter. And if he were ever to sport an earring, she was sure that he would somehow do so with style.

"So, you found an earring," Mma Ramotswe said. "Did you ask your husband about it?"

"Of course not," said Mma Modise. "He would deny it. Men never confess to these things."

Mma Ramotswe made up her mind. "I'll have to think about this, Mma. Could I let you know in a day or two whether I can do what you ask of me?"

Mma Modise nodded. "I hope the answer will be yes, Mma." She fixed Mma Ramotswe with a challenging stare. Now came the emotional appeal: "We women, you see, must stick together, Mma Ramotswe. My husband has plenty of people to go to—all the men at his football club, all his friends in the pest control business. Who have I got, Mma? Nobody. I have nobody."

Mma Ramotswe felt the weight of the plea lie heavily on her.

Then she thought: What about her brother? Had Mma Modise not got an attentive brother—a broad enough shoulder for her to lean upon? Now she said, tentatively, "Your brother, Mma . . ."

It was as if Mma Modise had not heard her. "Just you, Mma. I am asking you, Mma. Your sign out there says, *For the problems of ladies and others*. I am a lady with a problem. My husband is that problem. I am just one of hundreds of women—no, thousands—for whom their husband is a big problem."

It was a direct request—and an unashamed appeal to the solidarity of women. It would be difficult to say no, thought Mma Ramotswe. And it became even more difficult after Mma Modise said, "Sisters must help one another. I'm sure you agree with that, Mma."

With a growing sense of being trapped, Mma Ramotswe realised that she was now faced with the prospect of acting for two clients at the same time, each interested in finding out something about the other. These were uncharted waters for her, although one thing, at least, was certain: Clovis Andersen would never have allowed himself to get into such a position. But then Clovis Andersen was a man, and it was easier for him. He did not have to deal with the claims of sisterhood—claims to which it was difficult for any woman to be indifferent.

THAT EVENING, Mma Ramotswe and Mr. J.L.B. Matekoni sat on the verandah of their house on Zebra Drive, watching the last of the light fade from the sky. It was a still time—a time when the world seemed to wind down from the exertions of the day, a time of homecoming, a time for reflection, even if that reflection was on as simple a matter as what was for dinner. It was important, Mma Ramotswe believed, to devote to the small things of life the same thought and consideration as one gave to the large. And so, if you found yourself thinking about the issue of whether you had prepared enough beans for the pot, or whether the roast chicken might stretch to two meals rather than one, there was no need to tell yourself that you should be thinking bigger, more elevated thoughts. There would always be time for those later on, although it was important, as a general rule, not to put them off until it was too late. Do not wait until it is your last day or two on this earth to stop and gaze at the sky, to breathe in the morning air, to be grateful for the simple fact of being alive. Do not leave these things undone, she thought, because none of us knows when we might suddenly find that we do not have the time to do them all—or the time to say to others the things that we should have said a long time earlier—such as *I'm so sorry* or *I love you so much, and always have*, or other things about which we might feel embarrassment. Sitting on the verandah with Mr. J.L.B. Matekoni, she thought about these things, and for a few moments was worried about the beans she had set aside for dinner, until he turned to her and said, "I saw Mogorosi again today. He dropped by at the garage to have a chat."

"Freddie Mogorosi?" she asked, forgetting about the beans: they would do, she decided.

"Yes. He came to see me when you were out with Charlie in your van." He paused, and gave Mma Ramotswe a sideways glance, as one might do when raising a subject known to be controversial. They had talked about the van on a number of occasions recently, when Mr. J.L.B. Matekoni had raised, as tactfully and allusively as he could, the possibility of replacing the tiny white van with something more modern. This he had done in as positive a way as he could, mentioning the various mechanical improvements that had been made in the design of even the humblest vehicles. Central locking, for instance, had been a giant leap forward, as a driver could now lock two or more doors with a single action. Was Mma Ramotswe interested in that?

The answer, given immediately, and in a slightly defensive, if not puzzled tone, was that she was not. "Why would anybody want to save time over such a small thing?" she asked. "And what if you wanted to lock only one door and leave the other door unlocked?"

He had said, "But why would anybody want to do that, Mma? Who leaves one door of a vehicle unlocked while the other is secured?"

She thought about that, and had to admit she could not imagine any circumstance in which somebody might wish to do that. At the same time, she felt that there must be few people who were so busy that they did not have time to walk round to the other side of a car and lock or unlock the door. "We must not allow ourselves to become too lazy," she said. "We are getting to the point where we expect machines to do everything for us, Mr. J.L.B. Matekoni. I know that you like machines, but there are limits, I think. Will we be expecting machines to do our breathing for us in future? Will we expect to have machines that can brush our teeth for us? That sort of thing?"

He considered this for a few moments, and eventually said, "But Mma, have you not seen these electric toothbrushes? They are exactly that. They are machines that clean our teeth."

The conversation had not gone further, but the issue of the future of the tiny white van was one that remained there in the background. She accepted that one day it might have to be replaced, but that day was yet to come. Yet when the van was mentioned, as it was now, he felt it wise to move the conversation on to safer ground.

"So, what did Mogorosi have to say, Rra? Was there anything important—or was it just a general chat?"

Mr. J.L.B. Matekoni took a sip of the cold beer that he liked to have when they sat together before dinner. And Mma Ramotswe turned to her red bush tea.

He answered, "It was a bit important, Mma. It was about this new licensing body they're setting up for the motor trade. The government has said that it's going ahead with it."

Mma Ramotswe was not particularly interested in the affairs of the motor trade. It was possible, she felt, to go through life without ever thinking of the motor trade—there were many people, of course, who did just that—but she nonetheless nodded in response to this news and asked him what he thought of it.

"I think it's a good idea," he said. "We don't want any riff-raff coming into the motor trade and taking advantage of the public. If people need a licence to deal in cars, then that will mean the government can stop unsuitable people from taking advantage of people."

"That sounds wise," said Mma Ramotswe, beginning to think about beans again.

But then came more significant news. "Mogorosi has said he would like to put my name down to be a member of the licensing board. They are wanting to have a member from the trade itself. The rest of the members will be from government departments."

Mma Ramotswe digested this. She could think of no particular objection to his doing this, and of course if he took it up, he would show all the conscientiousness that he showed in his work at the garage. But did he want to take on something that would presumably eat into his spare time?

"What do you think, Mr. J.L.B. Matekoni?" she asked. "Is it something you *want* to do?"

"I suppose so," he said. "Mogorosi was very persuasive. He said that I owed it to the country."

Mma Ramotswe smiled. "That's a bit much, don't you think? And why can't Mogorosi put his own name forward? He's a big figure in the motor trade, isn't he?"

Mr. J.L.B. Matekoni agreed that Mr. Freddie Mogorosi counted for something in the trade, and yes, he would be an obvious candidate for appointment. "But I think he's too shy," he said. "That must be the reason why he doesn't want it to be him. Some people don't like the limelight, Mma—it's just the way they are. They are like mushrooms, maybe—they prefer the shade."

Mma Ramotswe blinked. A mushroom? According to Mma Makutsi, who had met him during his first visit, Mr. Freddie Mogorosi was annoyingly loud. Would a mushroom speak—if it were to speak—in a booming voice? How had Mma Makutsi put it: *like a teacher shouting at unruly children*? She thought not. A mushroom, if it were to be vocal, would utter no more than a soft, mushy whisper . . . rather like the voice she imagined Mma Makutsi's shoes used . . .

She looked dubious. "From what Mma Makutsi said, he doesn't sound all that shy. She said that he has a very loud voice. That was just her view, of course, but that was what she said."

Mr. J.L.B. Matekoni looked away. "You know how Grace can be, Mma. She gets these ideas about people."

Mma Ramotswe waited, but he did not seem ready to expand on what he had said. "Possibly—" she began.

He interrupted her. "But she does, Mma. You've seen it. I've seen it. We've all seen it. Mma Makutsi decides that she doesn't approve of somebody, and that's that. They don't stand a chance."

She had to admit that there was some truth in what he said. Mma Makutsi was a woman of firm views, and was not known for her flexibility. On the other hand, some of her positions had mellowed, her attitude towards Charlie being an example of just that. And there were other examples that pointed to the exercise of greater tolerance on her part. Not that one would want Mma Makutsi to become *too* tolerant. There was a place for people who stood by their convictions when others were bending with the wind, and Mma Makutsi was certainly such a person. She was a rock, to use the term that some people used in such circumstances.

Mma Ramotswe glanced at her husband. She did not want to hurt his feelings. Men found friendships much more difficult than women did—she had always felt that—and she should be pleased that he had been able to make a new friend. Even if Mr. Freddie Mogorosi might not be her first choice of a friend for him, she should be careful not to give the impression that she disapproved. After all, they must have a certain amount in common—they were both obviously interested in cars, and even if Mr. J.L.B. Matekoni had little fishing experience, the idea of setting off in a boat in pursuit of fish must appeal to some deep masculine desire to go off in search of food. Boys will insist on being boys, she said to herself—and smiled at the thought.

"You are thinking something funny, Mma?" he asked.

She was careful. "No . . . well, yes. I was thinking: Why do men seem to like fishing more than women do? What's the reason for that, Rra?"

He shrugged. "Because women have better things to do, Mma?"

They both laughed. If there had been tension in the air, occasioned by the mention of Mr. Freddie Mogorosi, it quickly disappeared. The friends of others, she thought, are not necessarily the friends we would choose ourselves; that was one of the great consolations of friendship—it was a matter of personal choosing. Our parents should not choose our friends for us—we saw through any such attempts when we were very young—nor should our spouses.

Now they could both sit back and enjoy the final moments of dusk before it slipped into darkness. A bird flew across the sky: a quick dart of movement that disappeared into the foliage of a tree. There was a whiff of smoke on the air, just a hint, as somewhere somebody made a fire in the night. There were stars, fields of them, and a sliver of moon hanging over the great Kalahari, watchful, understanding.

CHAPTER NINE

BIG, BIG DANGER

THE PREDOMINANT COLOUR was brown, but then there was a green that was more brown than green, and the pale blue of the sky and the water. And all of these shimmered in the growing heat of the day, so that brown and green and blue merged at the edges.

Mr. Freddie Mogorosi had picked up Mr. J.L.B. Matekoni in his expensive off-road vehicle, a creature of high, wide tyres and resilient suspension, a cocoon of cooled-down air and purring machinery. It was light years away from the old green truck that stood outside Tlokweng Road Speedy Motors, ready to rescue stranded cars from roadside and ditch. But if there were those who might feel envious of this new and expensive piece of engineering, they did not include Mr. J.L.B. Matekoni, a mechanic of the old school and not, in his words, "a computer operator with grease on his hands." He still knew how to coax machinery into life; he still knew how to listen to the sound an engine was making and reach a diagnosis on the basis of what it told you, and not rely, as modern mechanics did, on some expensive piece of equipment picking up the signals from inaccessible sensors. So, while he understood why some would like vehicles like that in which he was travelling to the dam with his friend, he was content with what he had and knew.

"Do you like my wheels?" Mr. Mogorosi asked, as they began their brief journey.

Mr. J.L.B. Matekoni nodded. He did not like cars to be referred to as *wheels*; he thought it somehow disrespectful. Wheels were only part of it—an important part, of course, but not the whole glorious creation that was a mechanical vehicle. "Nice," he said, and added, "The suspension feels very good, I think."

Mr. Freddie Mogorosi let out a whistle of admiration. "Very good? It's A1, my friend. You drive into a ditch, and you don't feel it. You think maybe there was a little stone on the road—something like that."

"That is good," said Mr. J.L.B. Matekoni, staring out of the tinted window of the passenger seat. Why did people like tinted windows? Why should anybody want to hide from others? It was understandable if you were a government minister, because people were always waving at you as you went past, because the electorate was always wanting something to be done about something or other, and those in power would have no peace if they could be spotted in their cars. Had not Mma Potokwane herself recently tapped on the windows of a ministerial car that had stopped behind her at a red light? By all accounts, she had stepped out of her car, walked back to the cowering politician and given him a piece of her mind about delays to repairs to some storm drain out at Tlokweng. He smiled at the memory. He could not imagine that anybody, even the most powerful person in the land, would be able to stand up to Mma Potokwane in complaining mood. The storm drain, he understood, had been fixed the next day, and improved into the bargain. That was the way to get things done: to shake your finger at those responsible, although you had to have the bearing and authority of Mma Potokwane to do it. He himself had never been able to make too much of a fuss about anything, as he perhaps was too ready to believe that those in authority were doing their best.

Tinted windows in cars were probably chosen by those with something to hide, he decided—just as sunglasses were worn indoors by people who did not want you to see their eyes. Those were definitely people with a secret, he thought—and he knew that Mma Ramotswe shared his views on that. They had discussed the issue once before, and she had spoken of a client who had insisted on keeping his dark glasses on when he came into the office. He turned out to be incorrigibly dishonest, and Mma Ramotswe had said that she should have realised it at their first meeting. "He did not want me to look into his eyes," she said. "Be very careful, Rra, of people who do not want you to look into their eyes. Eyes, you see, are bad liars. My late daddy told me that, you know. He said that he could see everything in a person's eyes—and in the eyes of cattle, too. Cattle, he said, do not lie, but you can tell when they have given up inside. You can always tell that, he said."

Now, as they drove out onto the Lobatse Road, he said to Mr. Freddie Mogorosi, "You have tinted windows, Rra."

Freddie Mogorosi grinned. "Yes, I didn't choose them. They were there when I bought this car, you see. It had very low mileage, but it had belonged to a man who was . . . how do I put it, Rra? Very successful with the ladies—know what I mean?"

Mr. J.L.B. Matekoni took a few moments to think about this. As a mechanic, he could not approve of some of the uses to which people put cars.

"I hope he was not . . . not being successful with the ladies while he was driving."

Freddie Mogorosi found this very amusing, although Mr. J.L.B. Matekoni was not one to joke about such matters. "I wouldn't count on it, Mr. J.L.B. Matekoni. And, anyway, you and I know that people get up to ridiculous things while they're driving. My wife puts on lipstick while she's at the wheel, would you believe it? She says it's perfectly safe."

Mr. J.L.B. Matekoni shook his head.

"Not a good idea," Mogorosi continued. "Mind you, she's a very good driver, you know. She did the journey between Gaborone and Lobatse in record time the other day. I asked her whether she had driven or flown a plane. She thought it very funny."

Mr. J.L.B. Matekoni bit his lip. He did not approve of speeding. There was a reason for speed limits, he felt—and the sight of the occasional wrecked car by the side of the road was a forceful reminder of that.

"I tell her that she is a fast lady," went on Mr. Freddie Mogorosi. "Fast lady, you know. That usually means . . ."

Mr. J.L.B. Matekoni nodded. He was not enjoying this conversation. So he remarked, "It is still very hot. We must get some rain soon."

"Oh, the rain will come," said Freddie Mogorosi. "Next week, I think. Maybe the week after. But it will come all right. And then the dam will be overflowing, I imagine. Or, shall I say, I hope. All that water. Good fishing."

The dam was now in sight—a shimmer of blue in the mid-distance, below the hills. Mr. J.L.B. Matekoni felt a touch of excitement. He remembered when he had last been out in a boat, some time ago, before he and Mma Ramotswe had met. It had been on the Limpopo, up near the Tuli Block, when he had gone up to service a fleet of vehicles owned by a safari company. He had been up there for almost a week, and on the last day he had been taken out on the river by one of the guides. They had got rather too close to a family of hippopotamuses and had been warned off by a large bull hippo with enormous tusks. He had not enjoyed himself and had been pleased to get back to the camp. The Gaborone Dam was very different, he thought, and an afternoon of fishing with his new friend would be a relaxing end to what had been a rather busy week.

"There," said Mr. Freddie Mogorosi, pointing to a shack at the edge of the water. "That's where you hire the boat. That's Baagisi's place."

"Does he come out with us?" asked Mr. J.L.B. Matekoni.

Mogorosi shook his head. "No. He sets you up with the boat and the equipment. Then you're on your own. You don't want Baagisi with you—he keeps going on about politics."

"About what?"

"He says that the government isn't doing enough for people who hire out boats," explained Mogorosi. "He says that everybody else is getting government grants, but there's nothing for people who hire out boats. He never stops—and the thing about fishing, you see, is that you have to be quiet." He broke into a chuckle. "The fish hear Baagisi going on about government grants and they keep well away."

They drove down to the shack. The boat, propelled by a small outboard motor, was big enough for three or four people at the most. It looked shabby, but serviceable, although Mr. J.L.B. Matekoni's practised eye took in the look of neglect that hung above the motor. But he saw, too, that there were oars in the bottom of the boat—which meant that there would always be a way of returning to shore should the motor fail.

Baagisi gave them an effusive welcome. He and Mr. Freddie Mogorosi clearly knew one another well, and engaged in animated conversation about the last fishing expedition that Mogorosi had embarked upon when a large catfish—the largest ever seen in the dam—had been taken in the deep waters near the wall. "They like it down there," Baagisi said. "But the big fish have been out in the middle these last few days. That's where you should be going today. Slap bang in the middle—big bream, four kilos and upwards. Big fellows."

Mogorosi listened intently. "Good idea," he said.

Baagisi looked at Mr. J.L.B. Matekoni. "You're in the motor trade too, Rra?"

It was Mr. Freddie Mogorosi who answered. "Mr. J.L.B. Matekoni is one of the great mechanics of Botswana," he said. "Everyone knows that."

Mr. J.L.B. Matekoni was embarrassed, but Baagisi was interested. "You have the ear of the government, Rra?" he asked. "You fix their cars?"

"Well—" began Mr. J.L.B. Matekoni.

"Because if you see those guys," Baagisi went on, "you might be able to ask them about when they're going to do anything for small businesses like mine. I'm in the tourism sector, Rra, but do they give me any support? They do not. And advertisements? *Come fishing with experts on the Gaborone Dam?* No, nothing. Any assistance for the upgrading of equipment? None."

"It's a great pity, Rra," said Mr. J.L.B. Matekoni.

"Pity, Rra?" exploded Baagisi. "It's more than that, I think. It's a scandal."

"I'm sure you're right," said Mr. J.L.B. Matekoni weakly. "The government shouldn't forget—"

Baagisi cut him short. "No, they should not forget. But do they? They do. Do they even bother to come down here? I'll take any of these government people fishing anytime, just to show them. But no, they can't be bothered to come down and talk to us. Not a sign of them—never."

Mr. Freddie Mogorosi glanced at Mr. J.L.B. Matekoni. His glance was eloquent: *See the problem?* it said.

THEY BOARDED THE BOAT TOGETHER, with Mr. Freddie Mogorosi sitting beside the noisy outboard motor and Mr. J.L.B. Matekoni perched somewhat insecurely on the forward thwart. Mogorosi had brought a tin pail in which was stored their bait, a writhing mass of earthworms.

Baagisi handed them two fishing rods. "These are very good rods," he said. "They have caught big fish every day without fail." He paused. "Are you sure you don't want me to come with you, Mogorosi? I could show you just where the fish are, no problem."

"You are very kind, Rra," said Mogorosi firmly. "But my friend here and I need to talk about motor trade matters and it will be easier if there are just the two of us."

Baagisi accepted this reluctantly, and stood on the bank, watching them as they drew away from the shore. "Be careful of—" he called out, but his words were drowned by the noisy thud of the outboard.

"What did he say?" asked Mr. J.L.B. Matekoni. "What are we to be careful of?"

Mogorosi seemed unconcerned. "Does it matter, Rra? People are always telling other people to take care. Take care of this, take care of that. They say that all the time. Perhaps he said *Be careful of the water*. Well, we know all about that—we weren't born yesterday." He laughed. "There are so many people warning other people these days, Rra. Don't they have anything better to do than warn people about things? That is what I would like to know."

Mr. J.L.B. Matekoni looked ahead of them. Once you were on the water, the dam, which was the main water supply for Gaborone and its district, seemed much wider than he had imagined. What was it? At least a mile wide at this point—possibly more. And if you measured it from one end to the other, he had been told that it was at least two miles long. That was a great deal of water, he thought, and if the boat in which you were travelling were to develop a leak—as boats sometimes did—then you would have quite some distance to swim in order to reach the shore. If you could swim, of course, which one could not count on. He could, because he had been taught as a boy when he had gone to stay with cousins up in Maun, where there was always a lot of water. But in a dry country like Botswana, there would be many who had never had access to any large body of water and who would presumably go straight down if they were to suddenly find themselves tipped out of a boat.

"Can you swim?" he asked Mogorosi.

"Can I what?" his friend shouted over the noise of the motor.

"Can you swim?" Mr. J.L.B. Matekoni pointed to the water.

"I am a very good swimmer," replied Mogorosi. "Swimming is no problem for me, Rra. You must not worry."

"I can swim too," said Mr. J.L.B. Matekoni.

"Then we are very safe," said Mogorosi. "There is nothing to worry about."

They were now a good distance from the shore, and Mogorosi turned and did something to the outboard. There was a spluttering sound, and then sudden silence. Mr. J.L.B. Matekoni frowned. Had the engine been turned off deliberately?

Mogorosi explained. "It is very important to be quiet," he said. "We do not want to scare the fish away. So, I shall row us from this point until we reach the middle."

Mr. J.L.B. Matekoni helped him to secure the oars in the rowlocks, and then moved aside so that Mogorosi would be in a position to row. As he moved, the boat rocked.

"Be careful," said Mogorosi. "When you are in a boat, you should move slowly. These things are a bit unstable."

Mr. J.L.B. Matekoni nodded. He was excited by the prospect of catching fish, and was imagining arriving back at the house on Zebra Drive with a bucketful of bream. Mma Ramotswe had said that she would be happy to fry potatoes as an accompaniment as she did not think that pumpkin went with fish. The children would like it too: Puso, in particular, had always enjoyed the fish fingers bought from the freezer cabinet in the supermarket. This was sea fish from Namibia, all those miles away, and he liked to eat it with baked beans in tomato sauce. That made too sweet a dish for Mr. J.L.B. Matekoni, whose tooth was more given to salty and savoury tastes, but for the boy there was nothing better, it seemed, than a plate of those beans.

Mogorosi rowed energetically, grunting with each stroke. "This is hard work!" he called out.

Mr. J.L.B. Matekoni thought that it would be easier to use the engine, but he bore in mind what Mogorosi had said about disturbing the fish. He was the fisherman—he knew—and so he said nothing. He noticed, though, that a wind had blown up since they had left the shore, and this was blowing the boat across the surface of the water. They had been heading for the centre of the dam, but now they seemed to be going further up towards the far end, although they were still being kept off the shore itself.

Mogorosi noticed this too. "I think I'll bring the oars in," he said. "Then we can use the outboard again to get us back towards the middle."

"Good idea," said Mr. J.L.B. Matekoni. Fishing, it seemed, was not quite as simple a pursuit as he had imagined it to be.

Mogorosi manoeuvred the right oar out of it its rowlock and was about to do the same to the other one when he lost his grip. The right oar slipped off the side of the boat, landing in the water. Alarmed by this, he struggled with the other oar, over which he similarly lost control. That, too, slipped into the water beside the boat with a splash.

The recovery of the oars would have been a simple matter had it not been for the fact that the wind now picked up.

"The oars are drifting away from us," shouted Mr. J.L.B. Matekoni. "Quick, Mogorosi—fish them out."

Leaning over the side of the boat, Mogorosi made an unsuccessful effort to grab an oar that was just beyond his reach. "They're not drifting," he shouted. "The boat's drifting. It's the wind."

It was at this point that disaster struck. Leaning over the side in a further, more frantic attempt to reach an oar, Mogorosi suddenly lost his balance and toppled, almost in slow motion, into the water. The boat rocked violently, but remained afloat.

Mr. J.L.B. Matekoni held on to the side of the boat, which, impelled by the wind, was now drifting away quite fast, leaving Mogorosi and the oars behind it. Mogorosi did not seem too perturbed: for a few seconds he had floundered, but now he was treading water with an air of confidence. "Start the engine and come back for me," he called out, adding, "No problem."

Mr. J.L.B. Matekoni clambered to the stern of the boat and examined the outboard. He had watched Mogorosi starting the engine, and he now gave the cord a quick tug. The engine coughed but did not fire.

"Give it a sharp pull," Mogorosi called out from the water behind them.

Mr. J.L.B. Matekoni tried again, and, as he did so, he noticed at the corner of his vision a dark shape slide off a sand bank some way away and slip into the water. In a dreadful moment of realisation, he saw that this was a large crocodile that had been sunning itself on the bank.

For a moment he froze completely. I am just a mechanic, he thought. I am just Mr. J.L.B. Matekoni of Tlokweng Road Speedy Motors. I do not belong out here. I know all about the engines of cars, but I know very little about this insignificant little two-stroke engine that is the only thing that stands between us and the most terrible disaster.

He looked up at the sky, but quickly looked back down again. There was no help to be had from that direction—there never was. And now the nightmare returned in its full intensity. There was a large crocodile somewhere in the stretch of water between their boat and the shore. Mr. Freddie Mogorosi was also in the water. That was where things stood. I wish I had never agreed to come fishing, he thought. I wish I were back at the garage, doing what I do best—looking after cars. Most of all, I wish I were anywhere but here.

CHAPTER TEN

A LADY WHO HAD SOME HENS

AT THE VERY TIME that Mr. J.L.B. Matekoni was on the water, struggling with the engine of the fishing boat, Mma Ramotswe was driving her tiny white van into the car park of the President Hotel in the centre of town. The President Hotel was a favourite meeting place of hers, and for years she had been in the habit of having lunch there with both friends and clients. The lunches with friends were long, drawn-out affairs, chatty and filled with laughter; the client lunches were more formal and restrained, but provided Mma Ramotswe with the opportunity to get to know the people whom she was helping. She had found that she learned more about a client during half an hour of lunch-time conversation than she would from several hours around her desk in the office. It was food that made the difference, she thought: people talked in one way over food, and in another when there was no meal in the offing. That was the way people were, and if she were ever to write a book on how to understand people—and Mr. J.L.B. Matekoni had once suggested that she do just that—then the title of chapter one would undoubtedly be "What you say about food, and what food says about you." "One day I shall write that book," she said to herself, although in the next breath she added, "Although I know I probably never shall."

That lunch time, she was due to meet Mma Modise and convey to her the news that she had decided that she could act for her in an inquiry into the behaviour of Mr. Excellence Modise. It was not a decision that she had reached lightly, and she still had some misgivings about investigating one client at the request of another. Had there been another private detection agency in Botswana, she could have dealt with the ethical issue by referring Mma Modise to the other business, thereby neatly avoiding any issue of the conflict of interest. But that was impossible, because there was no other agency like the No. 1 Ladies' Detective Agency. Some years ago a rival firm had started up, but it was no longer in business. The public had given their verdict on that: Why go elsewhere for help and advice when there was the No. 1 Ladies' Detective Agency in full view, especially since she and Mma Makutsi had gone out of their way to make it known that they were available to deal with the problems of everyone, and not just of ladies. It was all a question of how one read the title: "We are an agency predominantly staffed by ladies," they explained. "We do not just deal with the problems *of* ladies. There is an important distinction there." Of course, there were some members of the public who were impervious to these subtle grammatical distinctions, but there was not much anybody could do about that.

Now, as she emerged from the van in the President Hotel car park, she cast her practised eye around the other cars parked there. It was, she noted, the usual mixture—a ragbag of old and new, shiny and battered, comfortable and entirely functional—and she imagined that applied not just to the cars, but also to the *people* who had parked them there, and who would now be ordering their lunch on the verandah and the dining room of the hotel. Smiling at the thought of how people matched the vehicles they drove—they always did—

she began to make her way towards the hotel entrance, but stopped as she passed a large tree around which the car park had been built. Other trees in the area had a long time ago fallen to construction projects, but this one had survived—a symbol, perhaps, of the old Botswana, and its values—and remained stubbornly present in spite of all the new concrete and glass that the modern world brought with it. You could build and build until you ran out of energy and could build no more—the country, the old ways, the voices of those who had gone before would all still be there, however much concrete you mixed and poured. And she was grateful for that, because she did not want that old culture to disappear, because it was a good one, and it helped people to feel that they belonged and were worth something. That old culture said that it did not matter that you had very little property; it did not matter that you were too feeble to work; it did not matter that you could do little that was useful; what meant something was that you were a brother or a sister of all the other brothers and sisters who made up the nation. That was what counted.

But it was not this tree that she looked at now, but the woman who was sitting beneath it. It was a feature of the old Botswana that if there was a shady tree, and if that shady tree was close to a path or to somewhere where people liked to be, then a flat rock, a small boulder perhaps, would appear and be placed in just the right position for a passer-by to lower himself or herself onto it and rest, or talk to other passers-by, or simply sit and think the sort of thoughts that come to us whenever we sit under a tree.

She saw the tree, and the rock, and the woman sitting upon the rock—a woman in a blue dress, wearing a straw sun hat frayed around the rim, and cheap yellow sandals: a woman of traditional build—distinctly so—who was for some reason shelling beans into a blackened pot at her feet. It was a village sight, this, but the boundaries between city and village were never all that sharp; one might easily see stray chickens under the bushes just yards away from a busy road, or come across small children, even toddlers, playing a dusty game in the shadow of a gleaming, tall building composed entirely of glass and sharp angles.

She realised that she knew this woman, and at more or less the exact same time, the woman came to the same conclusion about her. Yet neither knew how they knew one another, nor could recall what the other was called. That was typical of so many encounters in a place like Gaborone, a town not so large as to have become a place of complete strangers, as some towns now are. People still recognised one another in the street; people still knew where many of those whom they met came from originally, because, like so many towns, Gaborone was a magnet, drawing in those from outlying areas with its promise of the things that those small places lacked. So, you might still carry with you all the baggage of a village somewhere, a place where you had grown up with the same handful of people, where you were related to half of them, and where everybody knew all the details of the business of others. You took that with you to the town, and you discovered that everybody else had the same experiences in their past, and that you were still the you that you thought you might have left behind. And here was such a woman, thought Mma Ramotswe, who might have been sitting under a tree in Mochudi, if it were not for the fact that this tree happened to be in Gaborone.

The woman was the first to give the polite greeting. Then, when they had both said *dumela* and had made expected enquiries about health, the woman said, "Now I have started to remember who you are, Mma. I looked at you and I thought, I know that lady, and then I thought about how many years it is since I saw her. And I stopped counting, because nowadays, Mma, when you start to count years there are so many that it takes too long—it's like trying to count all the beans in this pot."

Mma Ramotswe smiled encouragingly. "I was thinking much the same thing, Mma. I was thinking that I was sure that this lady is from Mochudi, and we knew one another then, and that I used to see her . . ." She paused. It was coming back; it only needed a little time. "That I used to see her when I walked to school and I was just this high, no bigger, and—"

The woman shrieked with delight, and took up from Mma Ramotswe, "And I had a donkey that belonged to my aunt—it was a very old donkey, remember, and it had trouble with its eyes—and there was the cart that the donkey would pull and we would sometimes take a sack of flour from my father's store on the cart to the bakery behind the hospital. Do you remember that, Precious?"

The name had come to her, and now her name, which was Beauty, came to Mma Ramotswe too. "I do, Beauty," said Mma Ramotswe. "I remember all of those things."

They looked at one another in silence, reflecting on the years between them.

"And now?" asked Mma Ramotswe.

Beauty put down the bag of beans that she had been shelling. "Now, I live here in Gaborone, in Old Naledi. I have a dress-making business and a husband who is a bus driver. That is me, Mma. And I am sitting here because I have to go to the post office later on to collect a parcel. I am killing time, Mma, and then . . . and then what happens? I meet my old friend Precious Ramotswe and all the years disappear like that . . . gone in a moment. We are two young girls again, back in Mochudi."

Mma Ramotswe clapped her hands together. "It is wonderful, Mma. We are still here. That is very good, I think."

Beauty pointed to a smaller rock a few feet away, and invited Mma Ramotswe to sit down. "Just for a few minutes, Mma. Just to talk about those old days before we forget all about them."

"I am not going to forget them," said Mma Ramotswe, as she lowered herself onto the rock—gingerly, as it had been fully in the sun and was very warm.

"No, maybe not." Beauty paused. "And your daddy, Mma? I heard that he is late now."

"He is late, Mma. He has been late for some time."

Beauty inclined her head. "He was a kind man, your daddy. And he knew so much about cattle. There was nobody who knew more about cattle, I think. He was the man."

"He loved cattle," said Mma Ramotswe. "And I think that cattle loved him back. They never tried to run off when he came up to them."

"That is a sign," said Beauty. "Cattle always know when there is somebody who understands them."

They talked about people—about those who had been at school together, and about those who were still in Mochudi. And then Mma Ramotswe said, "I remember your grandmother, Mma. She was the one who told us stories."

Beauty laughed. "That is what grandmothers do, Mma. They tell stories."

"I loved her stories," said Mma Ramotswe.

Beauty looked thoughtful. "I was remembering one the other day. I was looking after my neighbour's child for the afternoon, and I remembered the story that my grandmother told me more than once—the story about the lady who had chickens. Do you remember that one, Mma? I told the child that story and she liked it. She asked me to tell it to her again, and again after that. You know how children are—they like everything to be done time and time again."

Mma Ramotswe smiled. "They are all like that." Then she said, "Remind me of that story, Mma. There are so many of these grandmothers' stories."

Beauty leaned back, clasping her knees with her hand. "The hen story? Why not, Mma, if you are not in too much of a hurry."

Mma Ramotswe glanced at her watch. She was not due to meet Mma Modise for another ten minutes. There was time.

"So, Mma," began Beauty, "there was a lady who had some very fine hens. These hens were very good at laying eggs, and every day they gave this lady at least a dozen. The eggs had very dark yellow yolks, and they tasted better than any eggs that lady had ever tasted—anywhere. She had been everywhere—all over the country—Maun, Francistown, Lobatse—and she had never found any eggs that were anywhere near as tasty. She was very pleased with her hens, and always gave them very tasty food. She would go and dig for worms in the bush because she knew that her hens liked worms after their main meal. She bought maize for them, too, and kept potato skin and other special delicacies for their birthdays. She knew the birthday of each of her hens, and she recorded these in a book that she had.

"The hens were very happy. They were well behaved and had elected one of their number to be the chief hen. She was a very fine hen with red feathers and a good fat body. She could speak Setswana, which is not always the case with hens. She also had some English, but not many words in that language—so she spoke to the lady in Setswana when she came to count them and feed them.

"Now, one morning this chief hen came to this lady and said, 'Mother, we are very sad because last night a jackal came into our run and ate one of our sisters. She is late now, and we are very sorry about that.'

"The lady was most alarmed. She said to the chief hen, 'This is very bad news, Mma. I shall try to keep a look out for this jackal and if I see him, I shall chase him away with a stick.'

"The chief hen nodded in that strange up-and-down way that hens have. She said, 'The problem, Mother, is that this cunning jackal will only come when you are away. If he thinks you are nearby, he will never dare show his face.'

"The lady realised that this was true. But she had an idea—she said that she would go into town and tell everybody that she was going away for three days. But she would not really go away—she would sit in a cupboard in her house where she would not be seen, waiting for this jackal to come and try to take away one of her hens. The jackal would almost certainly come, as he had many friends in town who would have told him that the lady was going to be away.

"And that is what happened, of course. On the second night, while she was waiting in her cupboard, she heard the hens starting to sing outside: 'The jackal is coming, the jackal is coming.' She went outside and caught the jackal red-handed and saved her hens from being eaten. They were very pleased, and they laid her twice as many eggs as normal for the next three weeks. The jackal was punished, and sent back to his people in the bush. He could not help himself, because he was a jackal, but he now knew better than to take the hens of that very clever lady."

The story finished, Mma Ramotswe clapped her hands with delight. As she did so, she glanced at her watch and realised that it was time to go inside and meet Mma Modise for lunch.

"We could sit here all afternoon," she said to Beauty. "But I have to meet somebody."

"And I have beans to attend to," said Beauty.

They looked at one another and smiled. They would meet again sometime, they said, and then they could talk once more about those days that are now long gone, but that are very important to anybody who lived through them. Their world—their country, with all its stories—was still there, not just in memory, but, in sometimes quite subtle ways, all around them, a reassuring presence that gave the same comfort as a parent might give, just by being present, when darkness falls.

AT THEIR TABLE in the President Hotel, Mma Modise expressed her pleasure on hearing that Mma Ramotswe was prepared to help her.

"I'm glad you have reached this decision, Mma," she said to Mma Ramotswe. "And I think it is the right one." She paused. "I didn't see any reason why you should worry about acting for me, you know. After all, I'm the one who's in the right."

Mma Ramotswe sat back in her chair and studied the menu. She took in none of the details, though, as she was thinking about what Mma Modise had just said. It was all very complicated, and she was not sure that she would be able to explain to the other woman. There *was* an issue here. You could not simply relieve yourself of your obligations to a client just because somebody else comes along and says that the client in question is in the wrong. That applied, she thought, even if the person who makes that accusation is the client's wife. There was a whole fat chapter in *The Principles of Private Detection* about that—about how one should not accept the evaluation of others unless one could confirm what they said. Mma Ramotswe had her doubts about that: perhaps the answer was to be cautious, rather than to exclude such information altogether. And if, at the end of the day, one reached the view that clients were on the wrong side, that alone did not mean that one should not give them a chance to show that they were right. Excellence Modise may be having an affair, or he may not. If she declined to investigate, then Mma Modise would continue to believe that he was. If an investigation showed her belief to be unfounded, then that would be good for her marriage. She might be more positive towards him and the marriage might be saved, which would be in the interests of both of them, she imagined. One thing she had learned in the course of her career was that divorce was messy. If you could avoid it, and still be happy, then that was far better than experiencing all the trauma and upheaval of splitting up. That might be necessary in some cases—and hers, she reminded herself, was one of those, as she would never have found happiness with Note Mokoti, her abusive first husband. But that was an extreme case—there were many others where people could easily make a go of things rather than giving up and handing the matter over to the lawyers. The trick in each case was to know when there was a point to repairing something that was difficult, or whether the time had come to bring it to an end.

She thought about this, but did not follow up on what Mma Modise had said. And Mma Modise herself had other things to talk about, including the question of how Mma Ramotswe would go about finding out what her husband was up to, and when she would be able to start.

"I don't know much about how you people operate," she said. "But if you'll forgive me, Mma, I'm not sure that it would be a good idea to park outside the house again. I did see you, after all, and I saw you again at the tea place. Not that I'm criticising you, Mma . . ."

Mma Ramotswe smiled. This comment was fair enough: she and Charlie had not been as discreet as they might have been. "I hear what you say, Mma," she said. "I shall be very careful."

"Because I don't want him to know that he's being watched. I don't think he'd like that."

This was true, Mma Ramotswe said. People did not like to be watched—in general, that is: she had once come across a client who had become aware that he was being observed and who appeared to enjoy the process. He had been insecure, she decided, and had taken pleasure in the thought that somebody thought him important enough to be observed. She did not think Mr. Excellence Modise was at all insecure, although . . . She remembered his confiding in her his belief that his wife did not love him. That could be a sign of insecurity—or realism, perhaps.

"I shall be careful," Mma Ramotswe reassured Mma Modise. "I do not think he will see me. You must not worry."

Mma Modise looked relieved. "Good," she said. "So what will you do? How will you find out where he is meeting this flashy girlfriend of his?"

She spoke as if she was already sure about the existence of a lover. How did she know that the other woman, if she existed at all, was flashy?

Mma Modise appeared to pick up on Mma Ramotswe's doubts.

"She will be flashy, of course, Mma Ramotswe," she said. "I am sure of it. Remember the earring? It was a big one, Mma. It was the sort of earring that a very flashy woman wears. She will be one of those ladies who wear short skirts—very short, Mma, almost just a belt, no more—and lots of jewellery. Lots and lots of it. Everywhere. She will be the sort of woman who says, 'Come on, men,' even without actually saying anything. That is the sort of woman he's seeing." She gave Mma Ramotswe a challenging look, as if she was expecting contradiction. "And she'll be after his money, too, you know. That sort of woman knows that if a man is a big termite exterminator there'll be money in the bank. They know that sort of thing. Then they flatter him and say that they find termite exterminators very romantic people, and the foolish man believes them."

Mma Ramotswe made an effort not to laugh. Termite exterminators did an important job, because without them the termites would eat their way through the whole country, but there was a difference between being important and being romantic. Indeed, romantic people were often distinguished by the fact that they were of no use to people—or no *other* use, one might say.

"Well," said Mma Ramotswe. "If this lady exists—"

"Oh, she'll exist all right, Mma," interjected Mma Modise.

Mma Ramotswe held her ground. "That's something I shall need to find out for myself, Mma," she said. "If this lady exists, I shall find out more about her. Then we'll know whether she's a sort of Violet Sephotho . . ."

The reference to Violet Sephotho slipped out, as for a moment she had imagined that she was talking to Mma Makutsi, who would have appreciated the reference. She had no idea whether Mma Modise would know about Violet—there was no reason to suspect that she would.

But Mma Modise did. "Violet Sephotho?" she exclaimed. And then, more quietly, as heads at neighbouring tables had turned, "Have you had dealings with that woman, Mma? Do you know her?"

Mma Ramotswe nodded. "I do not know her all that well, but my assistant—I mean, my colleague—Mma Makutsi, goes back a long way with Violet. They were at the Botswana Secretarial College together."

"She's a shocker, that woman," Mma Modise continued. "I've heard so many things about her—" She broke off, and frowned. "Do you think she's involved with Excellence, Mma? Is that what you think?"

Mma Ramotswe was quick to assure her that she had no reason to suspect that Violet was carrying on with Mr. Modise. "I was just using her as an example," she said. "She's a sort of gold standard of bad behaviour. That's all."

It was almost as if Mma Modise was disappointed to hear that Violet was not involved. "It would have been good to have a name," she said ruefully. "Know your enemy, Mma. That way, one can be aware of what one's up against."

Mma Ramotswe did not like to hear talk of enemies. It was only too easy to label everyone a friend or enemy, but that only perpetuated division. There were friends, and then there were people who were not friends but who could conceivably become friends if one made the effort. "Well, I don't think we should spend any more time on Violet," she said. "If you start looking in one direction, you may miss more important things happening in another. You have to keep an open mind."

Even as she said this, an idea came to her. It came with all the suddenness with which obvious ideas may occur, unheralded and without elaboration. If she wanted to avoid a lot of fruitless watching and waiting, this was clearly what she needed to do.

She looked up from the menu. "Do you remember any of the stories our grandmothers used to tell us?" she asked.

Mma Modise looked puzzled. "Yes, I do, Mma. I remember some of them—not all of them, of course." She smiled at a memory. "My favourite was about a young woman who marries a lion. Her new husband looks like a man, but there's something about him that says *lion*. Do you remember that one?"

Mma Ramotswe had heard it, but it had been a long time ago. "She then discovers that he goes out every night . . ."

"Yes, and her brothers say to her, 'This man you've married—we think he has the smell of a lion about him.'"

It was coming back to her. "And they tether a goat in a place where they know he likes to walk," said Mma Ramotswe. "And they hide nearby and—"

"And catch him when he goes after the goat."

"The goat knows that he is a lion," said Mma Ramotswe. "Goats know these things."

Mma Modise nodded her agreement. "Yes, they do. And they put him in a cage. Yes. And then he starts to roar, and this is more proof."

Mma Ramotswe shook her head. "It could happen to anyone."

Mma Modise laughed. "Only in one of these grandmother tales, I think."

Mma Ramotswe became serious. "I've just been reminded of another story," she said. "There was a woman who had some very fine chickens that were being taken by a jackal."

"I see."

Mma Ramotswe told the story she had just heard from Beauty. At the end, she said, "In that story, Mma, a woman pretends to go away, and that brings the jackal out. That was how she caught him."

Mma Modise was silent. She looked up at the ceiling. Then she lowered her gaze, back to the table and to Mma Ramotswe sitting opposite her; and she did this with the air of one who has found something out by looking up at the ceiling. "Are you suggesting, Mma . . ."

Mma Ramotswe nodded. "I am, Mma. I think you need to go away for three days. Find an excuse—any excuse will do."

"I have a sister in Mahalapye," said Mma Modise.

"Then you should visit her," Mma Ramotswe encouraged her. "Sisters need to be visited regularly, I think."

Mma Modise looked thoughtful. "Do you think it will work, Mma?"

"It did in that story," said Mma Ramotswe. "And I think the whole point of those old stories is to show us what to do. Well, let's see if they really work."

Mma Modise looked thoughtful. "You are very clever, Mma. I can see why you are a famous lady."

"I am not at all famous," protested Mma Ramotswe. "I am just Precious Ramotswe of the No. 1 Ladies' Detective Agency—that is all."

"But that is a lot," said Mma Modise, adding, "At least, if you ask me."

They looked at one another. Mma Modise was pleased with the outcome of this lunch—even before they had made their choice from the menu. Mma Ramotswe was less content; she still had niggling doubts about how this whole affair was developing. And yet this plan, hastily conceived, was probably the best way of determining, one way or another, whether Mma Modise's suspicions had any foundation. Now she made a decision: if it failed to produce any result, then she would withdraw from the matter altogether. She would inform both Excellence Modise and Mma Modise that they should patch up their marriage themselves and, if they were unable to do that, they should go to a marriage counsellor or a lawyer and discuss with such a person what could be done. She rather suspected that these two would eventually drift apart: that was better, perhaps, than staying together and being consumed with mutual suspicion.

A waiter appeared and took their order. Mma Ramotswe was determined that they would now talk about something different, as the business part of the lunch had been rapidly dealt with and needed no further discussion. So, she raised the subject of rain. Did Mma Modise think that there would be good rains this year—or at least a bit better than last year's? Mma Modise did. "I am an optimist," she said. "I believe that things will work out for the best—although I know that this often does not happen."

Mma Ramotswe thought about this. "But can you really be an optimist if you think that way, Mma?"

Mma Modise sighed. "I suppose not, Mma, but then . . ."

Mma Ramotswe reached out and patted her forearm. "No, you are right, Mma. It is still worth hoping for the best. That's the only way, because if you stop hoping for the best, what do you do? You don't bother to get out of bed in the morning."

"And that," said Mma Modise, "is something we all have to do. We all have to get out of bed in the morning."

With that fundamental question disposed of, there was no shortage of other subjects waiting for their attention. There was a new clothing shop that had opened near the supermarket on the Tlokweng Road. Had Mma Modise visited that? She had. And what did she think? She thought that there were some nice clothes there and she was thinking of returning to buy a dress that she had spotted on display. It was red, and she thought that it was probably her size.

"We are both traditionally built," said Mma Ramotswe. "It can be difficult to get the right size sometimes."

That was another subject for discussion, and it easily lasted until the time that the waiter delivered the lunch they had ordered. Then they went on to something else, and another topic after that, and talked about these things until two o'clock, which was the time beyond which Mma Ramotswe had always felt lunch should never be prolonged. Mma Modise agreed about that. In fact, they agreed about everything, as far as Mma Ramotswe could ascertain, which made her feel that she was doing the right thing in helping this woman. Mma Modise was in the right here—in so far as there were rights and wrongs in these matrimonial cases. Mr. Excellence Modise had something to hide—and she was confident that once his wife went off to visit her sister in Mahalapye, what he had to conceal would be revealed. She had felt doubtful earlier on, but now she felt much more confident about the likely outcome. Lunch could do that sort of thing: you might sit down to lunch in a state of indecision, and get up from it with a renewed sense of certainty, particularly if you took your lunch at the President Hotel, and if the chicken and rice that you ordered was perfectly cooked and quite delicious—particularly then.

They parted amicably. Mma Modise was pleased that Mma Ramotswe would be helping her, and Mma Ramotswe, for her part, was satisfied that she could respond positively to what was clearly a sincere cry for help. And yet, there was something niggling at the back of her mind: Why had the gardener been so dismissive of Mma Modise? Why did he have such a negative view of her—so much so that he'd confessed that he would have been happy to see her gate knocked completely over? That was, admittedly, strange, but there was probably a rational explanation. Many men disliked taking orders from a woman. It was an old-fashioned view, certainly, but you still encountered it. Perhaps the gardener was one of those men, and his reservations could be ignored as ill-concealed spleen. That was possible—indeed, probable, she thought—and she decided now to assume that to be so. The gardener could simply be ignored.

CHAPTER ELEVEN

GOVERNMENT CROCODILES

THE GABORONE DAM was an innocent body of water, not sinuous or mysterious, as were some stretches of the nearby Limpopo River. And yet, on the quiet surface of that dam, in broad daylight, and in slow motion, the life of Mr. Freddie Mogorosi, prominent and prosperous figure in the Botswana motor trade, was now in imminent peril from the approach of a large crocodile. Mogorosi was initially unaware of the imminent danger, and was even laughing at the fact that he had fallen out of the small boat onto which he and Mr. J.L.B. Matekoni had embarked. He thought that all he had to do was tread water for the short time it would take for his companion to start the outboard engine and come back to haul him up into the boat. The outboard, though, was temperamental—as such things can be—and Mr. J.L.B. Matekoni was having difficulty starting it. He had seen the crocodile slipping off the sand bank, while Mogorosi had not. And now he had to decide what to do.

As Mr. J.L.B. Matekoni struggled with the outboard pull-cord, he shouted out a warning, as loudly as he could, but still, as a result of the circumstances, in a wavering voice.

Mr. Freddie Mogorosi was splashing about and did not hear what was said.

"A crocodile," repeated Mr. J.L.B. Matekoni. "It's coming, Rra. A crocodile!"

Mogorosi suddenly stopped moving. Then his head disappeared under water, and for an awful moment Mr. J.L.B. Matekoni thought that his companion had been taken. That is exactly how it happened—when crocodiles were involved. The prey, animal or human, would have its head above water, and the next moment it would disappear. Sometimes there would be a desperate commotion just beneath the surface; on other occasions it would be as if there had never been anything there: a scene of undisturbed peace. Had this happened now? His heart gave a lurch. It was all so sudden, so inconceivable. Mogorosi gone . . .

But it was only momentary fright that had caused Mogorosi to submerge. Now, as he broke the surface, he struck out for the drifting boat with all the speed he could muster. At the same time, as Mr. J.L.B. Matekoni tugged at the outboard pull-cord with renewed and desperate vigour, the engine sprang into life.

"I'm coming now!" Mr. J.L.B. Matekoni shouted. "Don't worry!"

It took only a few seconds for the boat to reach the stricken swimmer. Now a bit more used to the engine and its contrary behaviour, Mr. J.L.B. Matekoni throttled back and slipped the gear lever into neutral, allowing the boat to drift the last few yards to Mogorosi's side. "You are safe now," he said, as he reached down to get hold of the swimmer's arms.

With a frightened backwards glance at the surface of the water behind him, Mogorosi tried to pull himself up over the side of the boat. This caused the boat to tip violently, almost spilling Mr. J.L.B. Matekoni into the water. There were shouts and splashing. Not far away, breaking the surface of the water, the head of the crocodile could now be seen. It was moving slowly, biding its time out of ancient habit: crocodiles can wait until exhaustion makes their target weary.

Mr. J.L.B. Matekoni made a quick decision. "Hold on to the side," he shouted. "But don't try to climb in."

Mogorosi was not in any mood to argue. As he gripped the side of the boat, Mr. J.L.B. Matekoni engaged the engine, turning the boat back towards the shore. Then, satisfied that Mogorosi had a good grip, he opened the throttle. The boat's prow rose as it made way under the burden of its bedraggled hitchhiker. But the engine, for all its faults, was powerful enough for the task.

Seeing its prey disappearing, the crocodile slid through the water behind them, its great tail providing powerful propulsion. Mr. J.L.B. Matekoni, glancing over his shoulder, saw the creature gaining on them, and coaxed an extra burst of power from the outboard. Now they were just a few yards from the shore and they felt the hull bump against rock. Able at last to stand up, Mogorosi let go of the side of the boat and began to stagger ashore.

Only to stumble. Down he went, and the crocodile, sensing its chance, shot forward through the shallow water.

Mr. J.L.B. Matekoni gasped. If the crocodile reached Mogorosi in the shallows, it would have no difficulty in dragging him back into the depths. And it would have done that, had Mr. J.L.B. Matekoni not seized the first object that came to hand inside the boat—a large, empty fuel can. Although this was heavy, the urgency of the situation lent him strength, as he hurled the can towards the approaching danger. Luck was on Mr. J.L.B. Matekoni's side: his throw was accurate enough for the can to land squarely on the half-exposed, half-submerged head of the crocodile. This was sufficient to confuse and frighten the creature, perhaps even momentarily to stun it, and it ended the attack. In a churning of muddy water, the crocodile returned to the deeper water, leaving Mogorosi to complete his brief journey in safety.

"Oh my goodness, Rra," said the dripping figure. "That was very close."

Mr. J.L.B. Matekoni found that he was shaking. He was a mild man, and rescuing others from crocodiles was not something that he had ever envisaged having to do.

Mogorosi came up to him and put his wet arms about him in a grateful hug. "You saved my life, Mr. J.L.B. Matekoni," he said.

Mr. J.L.B. Matekoni looked bashful. "Not really," he said.

"But you did," insisted Mogorosi.

Mr. J.L.B. Matekoni was silent. This had been altogether too frightening for him, and he wanted nothing more than to be back home, sitting on the verandah of the house on Zebra Drive, drinking tea with Mma Ramotswe and reflecting on the fact that between an exciting life and a dull but safe existence, he would, on balance, choose the latter.

From a distance, Baagisi had seen what was happening and now came running. "That crocodile is a big skellum," he said, panting from exertion. "That was why I warned you."

That was the warning they had not heard.

"Well," said Mogorosi, "thanks to this brave man here—" He pointed to Mr. J.L.B. Matekoni. "Thanks to this brave man, that croc has been sent away to think again."

"Yes," said the boatman, shaking his head at the effrontery of the attack. "I have written to the government about this crocodile. They wrote back and said it was none of their business. But I say that crocodiles *are* the government's business. If it can't protect people from crocodiles, why bother to have a government? No, this is definitely a government crocodile."

As they drove home, Mr. J.L.B. Matekoni imagined the conversation that might take place on his return. "Did you catch anything?" Mma Ramotswe might say. And he would reply, "No, Mma, but something almost caught us."

It was fortunate, he thought, that this response had occurred to him in advance. Witty observations like that required thought, and if they could be prepared well before delivery, then it was helpful, as the right words often came far too late.

MMA RAMOTSWE, not surprisingly, was shocked when she heard of the encounter at the dam.

"Oh, Rra," she said. "That must have been a very frightening moment—for both of you." She paused. "I am so glad that it was not you in the water."

He looked at her. "And I suppose I was glad too. But it was not very pleasant for poor Mogorosi."

She immediately regretted what she had said. "I didn't mean to say that I did not care about Mogorosi. I would not want *anyone* to be eaten by a crocodile."

"Of course not, Mma. I didn't think you meant that. I suppose it's just that when something awful happens, we are pleased that it isn't happening to us, or somebody close to us."

She nodded. "Thank you, Mr. J.L.B. Matekoni. But still, I am glad that nobody was taken by that crocodile." She gave him a quick glance, then looked away. She did not like to imagine that one day they would be separated, because nobody could live forever, and we all had to say goodbye sometime. Such thoughts occurred—we could not entirely banish them, but we could still resist them by thinking of something else, something more positive. She had always felt that this was the way to deal with doubt or despair—simply to crowd it out of one's head with thoughts of . . . what? Of friends, of family; of the sun coming up over the tops of the acacia trees and bathing Botswana with its golden light; of white cattle grazing on the sweet grass that sprang up so quickly after rain; of the rain itself, which kissed the land and brought life to it; of all these things.

She gave a shudder, and the shudder seemed to dispel any thought of crocodiles. But now she asked, "Is Mogorosi all right after . . . after all this business?"

"He did not seem to mind. He had mud all over him after he reached the shore—it is very muddy there. But he was very pleased."

Mma Ramotswe said that she was not surprised. It was very much better to be covered in mud than to be dragged down into the depths by a crocodile to be stored in those larders they kept under submerged rocks and logs . . . And it could so easily have been Mr. J.L.B. Matekoni . . . She closed her eyes and made an effort to banish the thought.

"The crocodile was very close towards the end," said Mr. J.L.B. Matekoni. "I managed to drive him off by throwing an empty fuel can at him. He didn't like that."

She shuddered. "Let's not think about it any longer, Mr. J.L.B. Matekoni," she said. "Let's talk about something else."

"We didn't do any fishing," he remarked. "We didn't catch anything—although something very nearly caught us!"

He had hoped that the witticism would have brought a smile to Mma Ramotswe's face, but it did not. It seemed that she did not even notice it, as she now changed the subject, to ask, "That business with the committee—has Mogorosi said anything further about it?"

Mr. J.L.B. Matekoni nodded. "He has put in the papers for me. He says that they only need to be rubber-stamped by an official in the transport ministry."

Mma Ramotswe thought about this. Why had Mogorosi put in

the nomination papers on her husband's behalf? Could he not have done that himself? And how did he know that the nomination would simply be rubber-stamped?

She felt that she should raise these doubts discreetly. She was becoming suspicious of this new friendship, but she did not want to be the prying wife who looked into every aspect of her husband's life. Mma Potokwane had once said something about that. She had expressed the view that men needed a certain amount of space, and that they resented women who insisted that they should know everything about their husbands' lives. That was understandable, she thought, as women felt much the same about their own private world. There were husbands who were far too controlling of their wives and who insisted on knowing every little detail of whom they spoke to, where they went, and what they did with their friends. As usual, Mma Ramotswe had found herself agreeing with her friend; Mma Potokwane was right about so much because of all her experience. From that little office at the Orphan Farm, in which she heard the stories of so many children and their families—stories that so often might make one weep—she had a glimpse of the best and worst of human nature. And that resulted, Mma Ramotswe thought, in the growth of wisdom. Mma Potokwane, quite simply, was *wise*, a quality that people did not talk about very much any longer, but was as important, surely, as it ever had been. Wisdom was something you could not buy, nor acquire quickly in any circumstance; wisdom was something that came slowly, after years and years of watching and thinking and weighing this against that. Wisdom was like dawn: it came slowly; it was a faint glow at first, and then, little by little, it filled the entire sky with light. That was wisdom.

"Mogorosi is very helpful, isn't he, Rra?"

She had intended that this should sound like an innocent observation, but that was not how it came out, and when Mr. J.L.B. Matekoni replied, his tone had become slightly defensive.

"He is a friend, Mma," he said. "Friends help one another."

"Of course they do," she said quickly. "And I was not suggesting that he should not help you in this. After all, he was the one who suggested that you should be a member—which was very kind of him, was it not?"

Once again, her attempt to conceal her suspicion failed, and it seemed that she was implying that Mogorosi's kindness was in some way excessive. Was it possible to be *too* kind? Perhaps it was, she thought. People who were too kind might be wanting something in return, and trying too hard as a result.

Mr. J.L.B. Matekoni frowned. "Mogorosi is a good man, Mma."

She inclined her head. "Of course."

"He does not want anything from me," Mr. J.L.B. Matekoni went on. "I think he is lonely. He likes company, but he has been so busy with his dealership and garage that he hasn't had the time to keep up with old friends. He told me, anyway, that a number of the people he knows have left Gaborone recently. I think he is trying to make new friends."

"I see."

The defensiveness continued. "And I do not think there is anything wrong with that, Mma. Do you?"

She was quick to reassure him that she saw no reason why one should not make new friends as one went through life. "It is probably a good idea," she said. "We lose friends, don't we? People become late—" She stopped herself. Crocodiles. Crocodiles lay in wait for the unwary. One's friends might be here one moment, and then the next in the jaws of some crocodile somewhere. It did not bear thinking about, and she made a mental effort not to do so.

"I am going to make dinner," she announced. "Roast beef. Potatoes. Pumpkin. Green beans."

"Oh," he said. "I am already hungry just thinking about that, Mma Ramotswe."

She smiled. "And afterwards, should we go and stand in the garden and look up at the sky? There is a very big moon at the moment."

He liked the idea. "We can do that, Mma. I like to look at the moon when it is full like that. It is like a car's headlight in the sky."

She thought about that. If you were a mechanic, as Mr. J.L.B. Matekoni was, that was presumably how you envisaged such things. She would not have chosen those particular words. She thought of the moon more as an eye—a great eye looking down on us on this earth: watchful, tolerant, and forgiving.

CHAPTER TWELVE

RAIN, MMA, RAIN

HEN THE FIRST RAINS CAME. Stacked up in the sky, from horizon to horizon, dark grey, becoming almost purple, dark clouds were the harbingers of what was to follow. A wind soon blew up, hot and insistent, and after that the first drops of rain. These were scattered initially, but within a few minutes became sheets of water falling like a curtain across the landscape, obscuring the distant hills, the broad sweeps of acacia.

People stopped what they were doing, pausing to look up at the sky, stretching out to feel on the palms of their hands those first drops of rain for which they, and the land itself, had so fervently longed. It was the same every year, when the rainy season approached; rains could fail, and did so with such frequency that people felt they could count on nothing. So, when the ancient promise was fulfilled, and the first storm arrived, people would want to check the evidence of their own eyes by feeling the storm upon them, by breathing in that very particular smell, the smell of rain meeting dry land. That was a mixture of dust and water and the electrical charge of the air; it was a smell that nobody would ever mistake for anything else. And Mma Ramotswe smelled it now, as she and Mma Makutsi left their desks in the office of the No. 1 Ladies' Detective Agency and went outside to witness the approach of the cloudburst.

"Here it is at last," muttered Mma Makutsi. "Rain, Mma, Rain."

"Yes," said Mma Ramotswe. "At last." And she thought of her vegetable garden, and her rows of beans that had been so patient in the dry months of summer and that now would respond with a burst of growth. She thought of the cattle, and of the way that they would fill out when the new growth came through, which it would, within days. She thought of the people in remote areas who had been obliged to harvest every drop of increasingly scarce water, and of how now they would have plenty, and could slake their thirst and wash off the dust to their hearts' content.

They stood outside, waiting for the rain to reach them. They could see it in the distance, its white veil descending from sky to land with the wind before it. Above their heads, the large acacia tree stirred in the stiffening breeze. A bird flew off, disconcerted, complaining, for thicker cover somewhere.

And then Mma Makutsi said, "Isn't that Mma Potokwane's car, Mma Ramotswe?"

She pointed down the Tlokweng Road to where a battered old car, unmistakeable even at that distance, was about to turn off onto the side-road that led to Tlokweng Road Speedy Motors and the agency's office.

It was Mma Potokwane, and her car drew up outside the office just as the first drops of rain splattered to the ground.

"You must come inside," Mma Ramotswe shouted to the matron as she emerged from her car.

"Rain!" shouted an exultant Mma Potokwane. "Rain, Mma Ramotswe! At long last!"

They went into the office. When the storm hit, they would be soaked if they remained outside.

"I was passing by," said Mma Potokwane, as she lowered herself into the client chair. "I'm not disturbing anything, I hope?"

Mma Ramotswe shook her head. "Mma Makutsi and I were sitting at our desks, Mma. We were going to write some letters, but have decided they can wait. And now you are here, and we can bring tea forward by an hour and have it immediately. It is always the right time for tea, I think."

"Of course it is," said Mma Potokwane. "You can never have too much tea."

"I shall make it," volunteered Mma Makutsi. "We have no cake to offer you, I'm afraid, Mma Potokwane."

Mma Potokwane chuckled. "That's a good thing, I think, Mma Makutsi. I am always eating cake and I know it's not terribly good for me. It makes me feel better, though."

While Mma Makutsi busied herself with the making of the tea, Mma Potokwane regaled them with the latest news from the Orphan Farm. A couple of new children had arrived from the north—a brother and sister who were nine and seven respectively, who had been found living in a wooden crate behind a butchery.

"It was just a box," said Mma Potokwane. "It had contained a quad bike and there was just enough room for them to sleep in it at night. They had made a makeshift door and a window, and had covered the window with a square of blanket for a curtain. That was their home."

"And food?" asked Mma Makutsi. "How did they survive, Mma?"

"The butcher gave them scraps," she said. "They swept the yard for him and chased away the village dogs that like to hang about butcheries. I think the butcher's wife was kind to them, but she had seven children of her own and could not add two more."

Mma Ramotswe observed that they would be much more comfortable now—and better fed, too, she imagined.

Mma Potokwane agreed. "Often children eat too much when they first come to us. They've been used to irregular mealtimes and when they find meals put before them at the same time each day, they are overwhelmed. They cannot believe that somebody cares about them enough to give them these meals."

Mma Makutsi sighed. She came from a background of hardship; she had sometimes gone to bed hungry as a child.

Mma Ramotswe said, "Those children are very fortunate, Mma."

"Yes, they are, Mma Ramotswe. The younger one still cries a lot, but that will change. Sometimes it takes a few weeks for a child's tears to dry out. But they usually do."

There was other news too, and a report on the pumpkins that Mma Potokwane was growing and that Mma Ramotswe had seen on her last visit. "They are getting bigger and bigger," said Mma Potokwane. "One of them is already the biggest pumpkin I have seen for a long time."

"They are going to like this rain," said Mma Makutsi.

They looked outside, where, through the office window, they could see that the rain had now arrived. And they heard it too, falling on the tin roof of the office and the garage, a continuous insistent drum beat.

"And you, Mma?" said Mma Potokwane, as she turned back to face Mma Ramotswe. "What has been happening here?"

Mma Ramotswe was about to say that life had been uneventful and that there was nothing out of the usual to report, but she stopped herself. There was something.

"Mr. J.L.B. Matekoni has a new friend," she said. "There is a man called Mogorosi—Mr. Freddie Mogorosi."

Mma Potokwane appeared to search her memory. "Mogorosi, you say, Mma?"

"Yes. He has a big garage. You will have driven past it, I think. The one near the hospital."

"Ah yes," said Mma Potokwane. "A big place."

"He is very successful, I think."

Mma Potokwane waited.

"He is being very friendly towards Mr. J.L.B. Matekoni," said Mma Ramotswe.

This did not surprise Mma Potokwane. "Mr. J.L.B. Matekoni is such a nice man—who wouldn't want to be friendly towards him?"

"He took him fishing on the dam," Mma Ramotswe continued. "Mogorosi ended up in the water."

Mma Potokwane smiled.

"And a crocodile took notice," said Mma Ramotswe.

Mma Makutsi now joined in. "This crocodile almost ate him."

Mma Potokwane looked alarmed. "Almost ate Mr. J.L.B. Matekoni, Mma? Oh, my goodness me, that is very bad."

"Almost ate Freddie Mogorosi," Mma Ramotswe corrected her. "Mr. J.L.B. Matekoni did not fall in. But it was a very dangerous situation, I think. Fortunately, they managed to get to the shore in time."

"That's a relief," said Mma Potokwane. "We had a child in our care once who had lost his father to a crocodile. It was very sad. He was a very brave boy. He tried to rescue him; he went into the water and pulled on his father's arms, but the crocodile was too strong. Those big crocodiles have a lot of strength."

"I am glad that nobody was taken at the dam," said Mma Ramotswe. "But I must say that I am a bit worried about this man being so friendly with Mr. J.L.B. Matekoni. He is trying to get him to serve on some committee the government is setting up. It's something to do with the motor trade. I do not think that Mr. J.L.B. Matekoni wants to do that sort of thing. I think that he has been pushed into it by this new friend of his."

Mma Potokwane frowned. "Men can sometimes get the wrong sort of friends, Mma. That is a known fact."

Mma Makutsi nodded her agreement. "Some men have no judgement. We ladies can look at a man and know straightaway whether he's to be trusted. I have always said that, you know."

Mma Ramotswe thought that was true, but felt nonetheless that there were plenty of fine men, and that these probably outnumbered the others. The problem was that men were easily led, and a good man might easily be led astray by one who was not so good.

Mma Makutsi had something to add. "I'm afraid that I formed a poor view of this Freddie Mogorosi person," she said. "And it was not just me: others took the same view."

Mma Ramotswe was unsure how to interpret this. Were these others possibly Mma Makutsi's shoes? She might have asked this directly, were it not for the fact that the office door opened and the bedraggled figure of Charlie came into the office. He had been caught in the storm and water from his soaked clothing was pooling on the floor about him.

"It's raining," he announced.

Mma Makutsi laughed. "So we see, Charlie." And then, scolding him for making the floor wet, she suggested that he stand on a piece of newspaper until he stopped dripping. Mma Ramotswe was more sympathetic: she rose from her desk to pour tea for the young man. "This will warm you up," she said, handing him a mug.

Mma Potokwane was interested in the committee. "What is this committee that Mogorosi has been talking about?"

Charlie looked up from his mug of tea. "Mogorosi? The boss's new friend?"

Mma Ramotswe was hesitant. She was not sure that she wanted to share her misgivings with Charlie. "I just mentioned him incidentally," she said.

But Charlie had something to say. "I heard that he has put the boss on some committee. Fanwell told me that."

Mma Ramotswe was silent, but Mma Makutsi asked, "What did Fanwell say about it?"

"He said that he was surprised that the boss was going on a committee. He said that he has always kept away from such things."

"He's right," said Mma Makutsi. "He has."

Charlie took a sip of tea. "I don't like that man. I've seen him a couple of times. I don't like him."

Mma Ramotswe and Mma Makutsi exchanged glances.

"Fanwell said that he thinks Mogorosi wants something from the boss," Charlie continued. "He says he can't work out what it is."

Mma Makutsi agreed. "Fanwell's right, if you ask me."

Mma Ramotswe was keen to move the conversation in another direction. The issue was a delicate one, and while she was prepared to discuss it with Mma Potokwane and Mma Makutsi, she was unwilling to involve Charlie. Charlie could be indiscreet—and it would be awkward if Mr. J.L.B. Matekoni heard that there had been general discussion of his private friendships. So she raised the issue of rainfall, and invited comments on how the crops would do this year.

"They will do very well," said Mma Potokwane. "I am very confident about the pumpkins I am growing. I hope that other crops do well for other people too."

"I think Mr. Freddie Mogorosi is up to no good," said Charlie, draining his mug of tea. "But I must go home and change into dry clothes."

He made his way towards the door, muttering as he left. Nobody heard exactly what it was that he said, although to Mma Makutsi, who was closest to him, it sounded like "Mogorosi, Mogorosi."

THE RAIN LASTED ALMOST AN HOUR, and was heavier than usual. The parched land was ready, and it drank in the deluge, but when the next fall came that night, much of it ended up as run-off. In the town, storm drains quickly filled, overflowing onto the roads, creating tiny lakes at intersections, slowing traffic, trapping cars. Yet by the time morning came, the excess water had largely soaked away and the roads were clear. All about, the land breathed again and tiny shoots of growth were already in evidence, so rapid was the response of the soil. Seeds that had hidden dormant until this moment burst into life; plants that had waited through months of dryness, tightening their leaves to preserve what little moisture there was, now brought a green tinge to what had been uniform brown.

The rain's impact on people was as immediate as its effect on the land. Under the weight of heat and dryness, people had seemed defeated, almost resigned; now they were animated, in tune with the freshness all about them. Mma Ramotswe was due to drive out to see an elderly relative in Mochudi, and was looking forward to the drive in these conditions. She was planning to spend the entire day out there, only coming back into town in the later afternoon. If there was more rain, she might return slightly earlier, but the forecast was that there would not be another rainfall for at least a day or two.

The office would be opened by Mma Makutsi, who had a number of administrative chores to deal with. No appointments had been made for any clients, and it was a day on which Charlie would be working in the garage, rather than at the agency. That meant it would be a quiet day—unless something untoward were to happen. Such days were always welcome—businesses always had a hundred and one things that were left undone until a day like this allowed one to catch up and bring everything up to date. With nobody else in the office, Mma Makutsi could even have the radio on in the background, which would keep her entertained as she worked.

At ten o'clock Charlie came into the office, wiping grease off his hands on a piece of the absorbent blue paper that Mr. J.L.B. Matekoni kept for the purpose.

"Just me for tea this morning, Mma," he said to Mma Makutsi. "Fanwell and the boss are doing something very delicate with a gearbox. They'll be on that until lunch."

Mma Makutsi rose from her chair to switch off the radio and start making the tea.

"Mma Ramotswe is up in Mochudi," she said. "There is that old aunty of hers up there. Her cooker has stopped working and Mma Ramotswe is going to sort it out."

Charlie nodded. "Actually, Mma," he said, "I'm quite pleased that it's just you and me this morning. I need to talk to you. It's a very serious matter."

He waited until she had made his tea. Then he said, "It's the boss."

She looked at him over the rim of her teacup. She had a good idea of what was to come, but left it to him to explain.

"This Mogorosi business, Mma," he said. "I've got big concerns. There is something not right."

She inclined her head. "I've had my concerns too, Charlie. You aren't alone."

"People like Mogorosi normally don't have any time for men like the boss. He's a big-time garage man—flashy showroom, shiny cars, *ya, ya, ya*. All of that. What does he want to do, listening to people like the boss who still talks about carburettors and stuff? These days it's all fuel injection and computers and so on. When did you last see a carburettor, Mma?"

Mma Makutsi waved a hand. "A long time ago," she said airily. She had seen something—and it might have been a carburettor, for all she knew.

"Mogorosi has money, and people with money tend to stick to other people with money. That's the way it works in life, you know."

Mma Makutsi shrugged. "Birds of a feather," she said.

"So the question I've been asking myself is: What does Mogorosi want?"

She waited.

"And the way I answer that question," Charlie continued, "is to ask another one: What has the boss got that Mogorosi might want?"

Mma Makutsi looked thoughtful. "What possession—is that what you mean, Charlie?"

"Yes. And the answer is right here: Tlokweng Road Speedy Motors. That is the boss's main asset, isn't it? That's where his money is invested. The Zebra Drive place is Mma Ramotswe's, isn't it? So that leaves the boss with the garage and his green truck. Nothing else, as far as I know." He paused. "The boss doesn't have any cattle, does he?"

Mma Makutsi said that she did not think he did. Such cattle as they had were Mma Ramotswe's—the remnants of the herd she had inherited from her father. "But you never know with cattle," Mma Makutsi continued. "Sometimes, people have cattle hidden away at some cattle post somewhere. You think they have no cattle, then suddenly they produce a herd of ten head and say that they had forgotten about these beasts and here they were."

Charlie agreed: cattle were easily concealed. But his concern was the garage, not any cattle that might or might not exist. "Mogorosi wants this garage," he said. "That is why he is seeing so much of the boss."

Mma Makutsi frowned. This did not seem to make sense. Why would the owner of a state-of-the-art modern garage want to get his hands on a tiny little business like Tlokweng Road Speedy Motors? It did not make any sense, as far as she could see. "And anyway, Charlie, Mr. J.L.B. Matekoni would never sell Tlokweng Road Speedy Motors. The garage is his life. It is all that he thinks about, according to Mma Ramotswe. It is always the garage, the garage, the garage." Charlie had the air of somebody who had a good answer to an obvious question. "Yes, Mma, it is true that this garage is very small. It is true that Mogorosi already has a big garage. But remember the position: this garage has a very good position. Many cars come this way when they are going out to Tlokweng. If somebody were to buy Tlokweng Road Speedy Motors and knock it down and build a big garage, then that would soon be a very big business, I think. Have you considered that, Mma Makutsi?"

She looked intrigued. "Possibly, Charlie," she said. "Possibly."

"Very possibly, Mma—in fact, more or less certainly."

"But what about Mr. J.L.B. Matekoni not wanting to sell?"

Charlie raised a finger in the air. He was enjoying this. This was his Clovis Andersen moment, when he revealed the explanation that would make sense of everything.

"I am now going to say something very shocking, Mma," he began. "I would not say this if Mma Ramotswe were here, but I can say it to you."

There was complete silence.

"Well, Charlie?" said Mma Makutsi after a while. "I am waiting."

Charlie lowered his voice—so much so that Mma Makutsi had

to strain to make out what he was saying. "That crocodile," he said. "What if it was Mr. J.L.B. Matekoni who was meant to fall in—not Mogorosi?"

Mma Makutsi stared at him. Was he really suggesting that?

"You see," Charlie went on, "if Mr. J.L.B. Matekoni were to become late, then the garage would be sold. So, I think that Mogorosi is just waiting for his chance. We have had the crocodile—and that did not work. Now there will be something else—and this time it might not go wrong."

Charlie finished speaking. Mma Makutsi had listened intently; now she shook her head in disbelief. "I do not think so. Oh no, surely not." It seemed as if she was trying to convince herself—and not succeeding, as she went on to ask, "Do you really think so, Charlie?"

Charlie's reply came quickly. "I am very sure of this, Mma Makutsi. I would not say this sort of thing unless I was absolutely certain. You know me: I am not one to talk loosely."

Mma Makutsi's eyes widened. She had never taken seriously what Charlie said about anything, really—her position had been to doubt it until otherwise persuaded. On the other hand, he was more mature these days, and there could be no doubt about the sincerity with which he spoke now, or about the gravity of the matter, as he saw it. But was all this based on no more than supposition—or did he know something that she did not?

"Charlie," she began, "you know about the need for evidence, don't you? You've heard Mma Ramotswe talking about this sort of thing, I think. You've heard her say that we should never just say what we think to be the case—we must have some grounds for saying the things we say. You know about all that, don't you?"

Charlie nodded. "*Ya, ya*. Clovis Andersen and all that stuff. I know that, Mma. One hundred per cent." He paused, fixing Mma Makutsi with an intense stare. "Since you asked, Mma. I can tell you exactly why I think Mr. J.L.B. Matekoni is in danger. It is because I know somebody who works for Mogorosi. He is a driver for his garage. He drives Mogorosi about, and sometimes his wife and his mother too. He doesn't like the mother. He says that she is always complaining that he goes too fast, and when he slows down, she complains that he is going too slow."

"And?"

"And he said, this friend of mine—we call him Big Nose because his nose is really big. He doesn't mind. He says people have always laughed at his nose and he's used to it. Anyway, I saw Big Nose last night in a bar I go to. He was sitting there, his nose sticking up—it always does. He was sitting there and I said to him, 'So how goes it, Big Nose?' And he tells me about this girl he's seeing and how she really likes him and he's having to fight her off because his mother hates this girl, and Big Nose has always been under his mother's thumb—" Charlie made a thumbs-down gesture, as if he were pressing down on a tack. "Anyway, he suddenly said to me, 'Your boss and my boss are big friends now.' I said, 'Yes, I had heard about that.' And then Big Nose laughed and said, 'If I were your boss, I'd watch out. I'd be very careful about where I walked.' Those were his exact words, Mma. *I'd be very careful about where I walked.*"

Mma Makutsi waited for more, but Charlie seemed to have finished.

"Nothing more?"

"No, just that," said Charlie. "But I think that's clear enough, don't you?"

Mma Makutsi looked thoughtful. "Could I speak to him?"

"You?" asked Charlie. "You'd like to speak to Big Nose?"

Mma Makutsi nodded. "I'd like to find out if there's anything more he can tell us."

Charlie shrugged. "I suppose so."

"Is he a regular at the bar you mentioned?"

Charlie said that he had not seen him there very often. "We could go to his house, though. He lives with his uncle, out at Mokolodi village. We would find him there."

"I think we should," said Mma Makutsi.

"And you should see his uncle's nose, Mma," said Charlie. "It runs in the family. Big? Massive. They call him Rra Nkô. Mister Nose."

"That's not really relevant, Charlie," said Mma Makutsi. "And it's not very kind to laugh at people's noses. They can't help it."

Charlie looked wounded. "I wasn't laughing, Mma. I was just telling you. If you don't want me to tell you things, that's fine. Just let me know, and I'll keep my mouth shut."

Mma Makutsi relented. "I'm sorry, Charlie. And thank you for telling me about this. We should go down there this evening. I'm every bit as worried about Mr. J.L.B. Matekoni as you are."

And that goes for us, too!

It was a faint voice—perhaps not a voice at all, although it seemed like it. Mma Makutsi looked down at her shoes.

CHAPTER THIRTEEN

WE MUST LOVE ONE ANOTHER

IT WAS WHILE she was driving back from Mochudi later that afternoon that Mma Ramotswe decided she would ask Mma Makutsi to accompany her to the Modise house. The previous day she had heard from Mma Modise that her arrangements were in place and that she would soon be leaving to visit her sister in Mahalapye. "I shall be gone for three nights," she said to Mma Ramotswe, emphasising the three. "In my view, three nights is long enough for a husband to get up to any nonsense he is intending to get up to—don't you agree, Mma?"

Mma Ramotswe replied that three days was more than enough. Some men, she thought, required considerably less time than that to get up to mischief: for many, a couple of hours was all that was required to go off the tracks. Many men were weak, and many of them found it hard to resist temptation. And women? Were they as weak as men, but in different, and perhaps less obvious ways? Mma Ramotswe was not sure about that. Women were more inclined to be faithful, she felt, as their main concern was often to protect the family, and to keep the home afloat. Men seemed to find it easier to follow a whim, to act impulsively and without much regard to the consequences. For the most part, women were more cautious in the exercise of their emotions. But then . . . then there was Violet Sephotho, who presumably never struggled unduly with temptation, giving in to it with enthusiasm, she imagined.

Violet Sephotho . . . Mma Ramotswe tried not to think about her too much. It was easy to whip oneself up into a mood of outrage over Violet Sephotho—Mma Makutsi often did that, becoming almost speechless in the process—but Mma Ramotswe was more controlled. There were people, she told herself, who were put on this earth to vex others in a whole variety of ways. Violet Sephotho was one of these, she decided, but that did not mean that one had to succumb to the urge to rant about her. Everybody knew what Violet was like, and a recital of her misdeeds would only have the effect of making one hot under the collar.

Then there was the question of charity, the topic of the bishop's comments at the Anglican Cathedral only last week when he had addressed the congregation the morning before the rains had broken, underneath those slowly turning ceiling fans, and with the children fidgeting in their boredom, and old Rra Mpho nodding off in his usual seat near the door. He had said, "If I am without charity then I am as a sounding brass or a tinkling cymbal." She sat up at the mention of the tinkling cymbal—it was such a vivid expression, and it seemed so right. There certainly were people who were tinkling cymbals; you heard them chattering among themselves, gossiping and laughing at some private joke—laughing uncharitably . . . She stopped herself, and looked out over the congregation. Charity was the theme, and here she was thinking uncharitably about these tinkling cymbal people, who were just like the rest of us, who *were* the rest of us. We *all* enjoyed a bit of gossip from time to time; we were all human. And then the bishop had said, "My brothers and my sisters, people sometimes ask me about charity, and about what it means. Some people think that it is all about reaching into your pocket and giving a few pula to some good cause. Well, that is one sort of charity, but there is a broader meaning of the word, and that is *love*. Charity is love that doesn't mind about imperfections and weakness; charity is saying that you *understand* what it is like to be the other person; charity is saying to others that it doesn't matter about their failings, it doesn't matter if they are wrong or labouring under darkness, that you still love them. Charity may be hard—it's not easy to love somebody who is cruel or selfish, but we can still do it—we *must* still do it . . ."

She closed her eyes. He was right; of course he was right. Because if we did not love others, we would end up disliking them, or shunning them, or, at best, being indifferent to them. And yet we had to *live* with them, and if we could not live with others then we would always be uncomfortable, even miserable, and there would always be discord and little fights and big wars . . . She opened her eyes. She saw that sunlight had come in through one of the high windows, and was on the white wall of the cathedral, a dancing patch of gold. That was what love looked like, perhaps: a dancing patch of gold.

She remembered this as she drove back from Mochudi that day, and the memory came to her again the following morning when she and Mma Makutsi set off together to call in, unannounced, at the Modise house. It was a Saturday, and she assumed that Excellence Modise would not be away somewhere, dealing with termites or some other pest. Would he be at home, sitting on his verandah, with his feet up, the other woman at his side? Or standing beside her in the kitchen, his arm about her waist, as she prepared a tasty lunch for the two of them? There were other possibilities, of course, but she did not like to think about them. This was not the side of her work that she enjoyed—anything but—yet she had to do it, because Mma Modise needed her help, and the No. 1 Ladies' Detective Agency should be available to everyone, and for *all* their problems—not just the easy ones. Every job that involved helping the public had its distasteful side. If you were a nurse or a doctor, you had to be prepared to carry out painful treatments; if you were in the police force there were times when you had to break bad news to people; if you worked in the cleaning department of the local council you had to collect food waste that had been left out in the sun and had gone rotten. All of these things had to be done as a matter of duty, and it was now her uncomfortable duty to intrude on Mr. Excellence Modise's privacy.

Mma Makutsi was more sanguine. She had picked up Mma Ramotswe's reservations, and set out to reassure her that what they were doing was unquestionably right.

"These men," she said, as they drove off in Mma Ramotswe's tiny white van. "They think that we women don't see what's going on. They think they can get up to all sorts of tricks and that we'll never notice. But we do. Oh, we notice all right."

Mma Ramotswe's reply was non-committal. "Maybe . . ."

"Not maybe, Mma. Definitely. Any woman can see the signs. I'll give you an example. There are some people who live near us. He's something in the government—not a minister, but very important in the transport department, I think. His wife is a headteacher in a school. She told me that she knew the moment her husband started to think of having an affair. She said that he bought himself some new trousers, although he never normally bought himself any clothes. Men leave that to their wives, you know, Mma Ramotswe. Men can be very lazy—although I am not talking here about Phuti or Mr. J.L.B. Matekoni. We are lucky because we have got first-class husbands, but many women do not have our luck."

"Perhaps—"

"Not perhaps, Mma. Without doubt. Anyway, this headteacher lady saw her husband taking these new trousers out of their wrapping and trying them on in the bedroom. She said to him, 'So you have bought new trousers—why have you done that? I am the one who always gets you your trousers.' And he said to her, 'I thought I needed a change.' Change, Mma? Change of wife, maybe? Was that it? She said, 'There is nothing wrong with your existing trousers. They are in good condition and they will last for many years more.' He ignored that, Mma. She said that he didn't say anything—he just got into these new trousers. Well, that was an effort, apparently, and they were so tight that he could barely do up the zip. He had to pull his stomach in and it was hard for him to breathe. What use is it having tight trousers if you cannot breathe properly?

"So, there he was in his tight new trousers, and when he took the first step, you know what happened, Mma? I'll tell you. The trousers split. They split all the way down one leg and up at the back. So this lady said, 'Look, your trousers have split! You can't go and see your new girlfriend with your underpants showing, can you? What will she think?' And the man looked at her, and she knew that she had been absolutely right, and he took off the new trousers and put on his old ones, and he said, 'I am very sorry, Mma. I have been a very foolish man. I am too old to wear trousers like that, and I am too old to have a girlfriend when I have got a perfectly good wife.' And she said that she understood, and that nothing more would be said about it provided he did not see this new girlfriend of his. And then you know what, Mma Ramotswe? The poor man said, 'But there is no girlfriend—I was just thinking of finding one.' Isn't that sad? Poor man. Whenever I see him out in his garden, I think of him standing there in his split trousers confessing that he had only been *thinking* of finding a girlfriend."

Mma Ramotswe agreed that it was a poignant story. "It is a pity that people try to be what they are not, Mma. It would be very much better if we all looked at ourselves in the mirror each morning and said, 'This is who I am, and I shall spend the rest of the day being this person.' If we did that, we would not try to be something we are not, and we would all be much happier."

"I think that too," said Mma Makutsi. But then, after a few moments' thought, she continued, "It is not easy for men, of course, Mma. They are often very lonely, don't you think?"

Mma Ramotswe was paying attention to the erratic driving of the car ahead of them, and she did not reply immediately. Then she said, "That's probably true, Mma. Men make their friends at work. They are not good at sitting about and talking with other men."

"How many friends has Mr. J.L.B. Matekoni?" asked Mma Makutsi. "I don't mean that rudely, Mma, but how many do you think it is? Phuti has one or two, but not many. He says that I am by far his best friend and that he doesn't really need any others. That is very kind of him, of course."

Mma Ramotswe gave this some thought. How often would Mr. J.L.B. Matekoni meet up with a friend? Hardly ever, she thought. Occasionally there was an old school friend, or somebody from the village he had lived in as a child, but that happened only very rarely and he usually said that he had lost touch with the person in question. But then there was Freddie Mogorosi and the burgeoning friendship he had with him. How did that fit into the pattern?

Mma Makutsi glanced at her. She was thinking of the same person. "This Mogorosi fellow," she said. "He's Mr. J.L.B. Matekoni's friend, isn't he?"

"It would appear so," said Mma Ramotswe.

Mma Makutsi sucked in her cheeks. "Have you thought of putting an end to that one?" she said.

Mma Ramotswe frowned. "Putting an end to it?"

Mma Makutsi was cautious. "I didn't say that you *should* put an end to it, Mma. I just wondered whether you had ever *thought* of doing so. That's all."

"But I cannot," said Mma Ramotswe. "And why would I put an end to that friendship, Mma? Mogorosi is his friend, not mine."

"Oh, I know that," said Mma Makutsi. "I was just wondering . . ." She hesitated. They were on awkward ground and she wanted to choose her words carefully.

Mma Ramotswe cut her short. "I think it's best not to interfere there, Mma," she said. "At least, that's what I'm doing—I'm not interfering."

"Quite right," said Mma Makutsi quickly. She wanted to warn her that Mr. J.L.B. Matekoni might be in danger, but she knew that this would sound ridiculous: Botswana was a peaceful, law-abiding country, and the idea that somebody like Mr. J.L.B. Matekoni, a mild, friendly, and entirely blameless man could be in some sort of danger, would seem so fanciful as to be absurd.

They were now near the turn-off that led to the Modise house. The conversation about friendship could be continued later on—if they decided to continue it at all. Now they had to prepare themselves for what could be an awkward showdown with an errant husband and his mistress. It was not a situation that anybody would pick for herself, she thought, but, as Clovis Andersen would put it, this was the way the cookie appeared to be crumbling.

"One thing that's certain about cookies," Clovis Andersen wrote in *The Principles of Private Detection*, "is that they crumble."

MMA RAMOTSWE DID NOT PARK on the road but drove decisively through the open gates of the Modise property.

"We are not hiding anything, Mma Makutsi," she said. "We are not coming here to look through any windows and then run away. We are coming here to knock on the front door."

Mma Makutsi was peering out of the window on her side of the van. "Yes, Mma, that is right. And the front door is open, I think. We may not even have to knock. We can go straight in and catch this man."

Mma Ramotswe switched off the engine. In the silence, they heard the ticking that an engine makes as it suddenly cools down. The tiny white van always made a rather loud sound, as if it were a clock that had just been wound up.

"I don't think we want to *catch* him," she said. "We are looking for evidence, Mma. We cannot tell him to stop . . . whatever it is he is doing."

Mma Makutsi glanced at Mma Ramotswe. This was a delicate situation—there was no evading that conclusion.

"What if he is . . . if he is having a private conversation with her, Mma?" she asked.

Mma Ramotswe rolled her eyes. "I hope that will not be the case, Mma Makutsi."

"But if it is? What then?"

Mma Ramotswe cleared her throat. "Let us worry about that if it happens."

They got out of the van and walked towards the front door. Out of ancient, embedded habit, Mma Ramotswe called out *Ko! Ko!* All sorts of standards might be in the course of being abandoned in all corners of the world, but she, Precious Ramotswe of the No. 1 Ladies' Detective Agency in Botswana, was not going to saunter into somebody else's house without properly announcing herself. And she would employ the correct greeting as well; she would say *dumela* to Mr. Excellence Modise even if she found him in the most compromising of situations. There was no reason, and no excuse, for rudeness.

The door opened rather quickly, and there was Excellence Modise—fully clothed, Mma Ramotswe was relieved to observe. He did not seem surprised to see them.

The appropriate greetings were exchanged before he said, "I saw you from the window, Mma, and your friend here, Mma—"

"Colleague," interjected Mma Makutsi.

Modise smiled apologetically. "Of course—colleague, Mma—"

"Mma Makutsi," Mma Ramotswe provided.

"Of course, of course. You are both very welcome, but please forgive me if I do not invite you in. The house is very untidy and I must put everything away before I invite anybody in." He paused, and gave a nervous laugh before continuing, "I wouldn't want people to think, this Modise is a very untidy man. I would not want that, I think."

It was Mma Makutsi who responded to this unambiguous message. "But, Rra, it is very hot, and we need to sit down and drink a glass of water. If we stand out here, I am sure that one or both of us will faint. We will go down like a cow under the sun, Rra. We must—" And with that, even before she had finished what she was saying, she moved decisively to push past Modise.

He was too surprised to resist, although he did utter one or two words of surprise. "But . . . but there is . . . but . . ."

Mma Ramotswe took advantage of the opportunity that Mma Makutsi had created, and followed her into the entrance hall of the house. And from there it was only a step or two into the living room, half darkened by the drawn-down window blinds. And it was in this room that they saw the woman they had been expecting to see, sitting on a sofa in a rather prim pose, an open magazine beside her. The woman looked up in what seemed to Mma Ramotswe to be genuine surprise.

Mma Ramotswe felt a momentary disappointment. It was not Violet Sephotho. It would have been such a bonus to have discovered Violet Sephotho sitting there. It would have been a confirmation of everything that they had ever thought about her. For Mma Makutsi, at least, it would have been the most natural progression from those early days at the Botswana Secretarial College when she had been so shocked by Violet and her behaviour, especially having just come down from Bobonong to the capital. But this was not Violet, even if it could have been.

Excellence Modise was at their side. He was flustered, and his voice was high-pitched and uneven as he spoke. That was a sign that he was lying, thought Mma Ramotswe. Untruth raised the pitch of the voice, even in an experienced liar. "This is our maid," he said.

This was too much for Mma Makutsi, who made a strange choking sound at the back of her throat. And even Mma Ramotswe, whose powers of professional self-control were well developed, opened her mouth in astonishment—and disbelief. What maid sat on the sofa in the living room and read a magazine? Maids worked in the kitchen—that was just the way it was, even in these egalitarian days. If they sat down, they tended to have a chair out at the back, just outside the kitchen door, where they could sit in the sun in between their household duties, and talk, if the house had other members of staff.

Modise sought to recover the initiative. "Please make tea for these ladies," he said to the woman. "It is hot outside, and they are thirsty."

The woman looked at him with unconcealed surprise. Then, like an actress who is suddenly reminded that she is on stage, she rose to her feet and mumbled some response. Mma Ramotswe watched her as she made her way out of the room in the direction of the kitchen. "I shall go and give a hand with the tea," she said. "Mma Makutsi, you can stay and talk to our host."

"But—" began Modise, helplessly.

Mma Makutsi responded quickly. "It is very good that the rains have come," she said brightly. "Do you think this will be a good season, Rra?"

She did not expect a reply, and did not get one. In the ensuing silence, she cast an eye around the living room. There was a display cabinet stocked with a collection of gold-rimmed plates. There was a picture of an eagle and a framed photograph of Seretse Khama, first President of Botswana and paramount chief of the Bamangwato. What would that great man think? Mma Makutsi asked herself. What would he say about all this?

She noticed the plush of the sofa, and the two matching chairs. The room was expensively furnished, even if in a taste of which she did not entirely approve. Phuti, she imagined, would describe the furniture as "over the top." He used that phrase about excessively fussy furniture—"It's too good to sit on," he said. "You must be able to sit on a chair. You must not feel that you have to stand because you're worried that you will not be good enough to sit down in a particular chair. There are chairs like that, you know. They are just for show."

Suddenly Modise found his voice. "Why have you come to see me?" he asked.

Mma Makutsi maintained her innocent expression. "It is Mma Ramotswe who has come to see you, Rra. I have come with her . . . to take notes."

His eyes narrowed. "Notes about what?"

"That depends on what you say, Rra," said Mma Makutsi, adding, "Although I am sure that Mma Ramotswe just wants to talk about business matters. You did consult her, after all."

"That is true," he stammered. "But . . ." His voice trailed off, and the silence returned.

Once in the kitchen, Mma Ramotswe said to the woman, "I am

sorry, Mma, but I did not catch your name." She had not been given it; this was a polite way of saying the same thing.

The woman looked away. "I am called Maria, Mma. That is my name."

Mma Ramotswe waited. People seemed to be unwilling to give their full names for some reason—it was an increasingly widespread habit. She could not say *Maria what?* although it was tempting to do so. Instead, she said, "I can help you make the tea, Maria. Where is the teapot?"

When no reply came, Mma Ramotswe repeated, "The teapot, Mma?"

Maria approached a cupboard and opened the door. It was full of foodstuffs—tins of syrup and of beans, bags of flour. There were no pots and pans, and there was no sign of a teapot.

"Wrong cupboard," said Mma Ramotswe.

Maria said nothing, but opened the door of the neighbouring cupboard. This was full of cleaning supplies.

"I don't see a teapot in there, Mma," said Mma Ramotswe, adding, "Unless I am missing something."

Maria mumbled something that Mma Ramotswe did not hear. She turned to a third cupboard. This revealed itself to be full of plates.

Mma Ramotswe moved forward so that she was standing directly in front of Maria. It would be difficult for the other woman to evade her gaze now.

"I do not think you are a maid," said Mma Ramotswe. "Most maids, I think, know where things are in the kitchen. In fact, *all* maids that I have ever met know what is in the kitchen cupboards." She paused. Maria met her gaze, and Mma Ramotswe could tell that she was frightened.

"I am right, am I not, Mma?" Mma Ramotswe pressed.

Maria drew in her breath. "You are right, Mma. I am not a maid. I am a friend of Mr. Modise."

Mma Ramotswe sighed. "I thought you were, Mma."

"I am visiting him," said Maria.

"I could tell that," said Mma Ramotswe, adding, "While his wife is away, of course."

Maria said nothing. She closed her eyes. It was clear that she was embarrassed. "I know what it looks like, Mma," she said quietly. "I know what you must be thinking."

Mma Ramotswe nodded. "I'm afraid that I was thinking exactly that, Mma. I am sorry, but that is all I could be thinking."

Maria now turned to her and gave a pleading look. "Excellence and I are not having an affair," she said.

"No?" asked Mma Ramotswe.

"No, Mma, we are not. I think that he would like us to, but . . . well, we are not."

"You have refused?" asked Mma Ramotswe.

"I have not refused," said Maria. "It is just not possible, you see. There are some men, Mma, who cannot have an affair with a lady because . . . it is just not possible."

Mma Ramotswe frowned. "You mean . . ."

She did not finish. "It is not his fault," Maria continued. "Sometimes these things do not happen. They just do not."

Mma Ramotswe gazed out of the kitchen window. She did not have much time, as Mma Makutsi would not be able to engage with Excellence for long. She racked her brains. There had to be an explanation. There had to be a reason why . . . And then it came to her. It was possible, just possible, even if it was unlikely.

She drew Maria aside. "We don't have a lot of time to talk about this," she said. "Do you know who I am?"

Maria shrugged. "You are some lady who knows Excellence?"

Mma Ramotswe lowered her voice. "I am from the No. 1 Ladies' Detective Agency," she said. "I have been hired by Mma Modise."

She had not told a lie. That was quite true.

Maria's eyes widened. "She spoke to you, Mma? She told you about all this? You're checking up on how things are going?"

Mma Ramotswe nodded. Now she would have to stretch the truth a little—but only a little. "She has told me everything."

Maria glanced over her shoulder. "It worked up to a point," she said. "I went to that bar that she said her husband likes to go to. He was very happy when I started to talk to him. Men love to be flattered—you know how they are."

Mma Ramotswe rolled her eyes. "Oh, I do, my sister. We all know how men are."

"I told him that I would like to get to know him better. He was a bit hesitant at first, but I really laid it on. Eventually he said that I could come and see him here, at the house. He would tell me when."

Mma Ramotswe nodded. "Just as Mma Modise planned."

"Yes. She would have told you about it. She is a very clever lady, that one—she knows how to plan things. And her plan went very well. I came here yesterday, and then again today. But, as I said to you, Mma, things did not go terribly well. You know what, Mma? I think that he feels guilty. I think that I managed to persuade him only half the way, you see, and then he thought better of it. That might be why he did not want to get to know me better, if I can put it that way, Mma."

Mma Ramotswe sighed. "Men," she said. She was thinking very quickly now.

Maria was anxious. "But will I still get my money?" she asked.

Mma Ramotswe assured her that she would. "I am sure Mma Modise will pay you."

Maria was relieved. "You know something, Mma—I am not one of those ordinary bar girls. I am not a bar girl at all. I regard myself as a therapist. I help men to come to terms with themselves. I have helped many men to be happier, Mma. It is good work that I do."

Mma Ramotswe said that she was sure this was the case.

"So, what now?" asked Maria.

"I think that we should all leave," said Mma Ramotswe. "Mma Makutsi and I will not need tea after all. We can give you a ride home in our van if you wish."

"You are very kind, Mma," said Maria. She paused. "You know something, Mma: I think that this man loves his wife. I really think he does. You can always tell."

"I think you are right," said Mma Ramotswe.

"That Modise woman is very wicked," Maria went on. "She does not deserve to have a husband like that."

"I don't think she does," said Mma Ramotswe. "I think you are a lady who understands these things very well, Mma."

"I do my best. I am not always right—not every time—but I am right more times than I am wrong, I think."

Mma Ramotswe inclined her head. "I think that when we go back in there, I shall pretend to believe that you really are the maid. I will say that I have remembered that I have to be somewhere else for an appointment and that we are going to have to leave. I will say that I have offered to drop you at your place."

"Thank you," said Maria. "That is a good idea."

They did as she suggested. After they had dropped Maria off, Mma Ramotswe and Mma Makutsi returned to the house on Zebra Drive, where they drank the cup of tea they had missed at the Modise house. As they sat on the verandah, Mma Ramotswe told Mma Makutsi about her conversation with Maria, and about how she had elicited the truth from her.

Mma Makutsi listened intently. Then, when Mma Ramotswe had finished, she said, "That poor man. He may be annoying but I feel very sorry for him." She paused. "Yes, poor man—with his uncomfortably tight trousers."

Mma Ramotswe gave a start. "Trousers, Mma?"

"Yes," said Mma Makutsi. "Did you notice how tight his trousers were? They were far too small for him." She looked at Mma Ramotswe as if she was surprised that such a detail could have been missed. "I noticed it immediately. I said to myself, Here is a man who is wearing trousers made for a much younger man. That is what I thought—my precise thoughts."

"Well, well," said Mma Ramotswe, and left it at that.

Mma Makutsi looked thoughtful. "One thing I wonder about, Mma: if he loves his wife, as he told you he did, then why did he get involved with that woman? That doesn't seem to make sense. Perhaps if he was worried about these . . . these private matters, then perhaps his self-confidence was low. Men can do strange things if they lose their confidence. They look for reassurance."

Mma Makutsi thought this sounded credible. She went on to reflect on the fact that they had misjudged Excellence Modise. He was not at fault here; it was his wife who had misled them. But she did not blame Mma Ramotswe for not realising this earlier. "We can all get it wrong," she said. "Some people get it wrong all the time. You don't, Mma Ramotswe. You get it right almost always, except when you get it wrong."

"It's kind of you to say that," said Mma Ramotswe. Mma Makutsi's compliments, well meant, of course, sometimes came out as veiled, or not-so-veiled criticism, but this was not a time to think about that; we all had our little ways—some more so than others, of course. But, once again, this was no time for such thoughts, and so she added, "Would you like another cup of tea, Mma Makutsi?" Tea was always safe—always.

"I would, Mma. There is so much to think about, and I find it is easier to think about things when you are drinking tea."

"That is well known," said Mma Ramotswe.

Mma Makutsi nodded her head in agreement. "If I ever write a book, Mma—and I am not saying that I shall do such a thing—but if I ever were to, it would be about tea and what it does for the world."

Mma Ramotswe said that this was a book that she would certainly read. "There are so many books we would like to read," she mused. "But one about tea should be right at the top of the list, I think."

Suddenly, Mma Ramotswe felt the need to add something to what she had said. "You know, Mma Makutsi, I am very grateful to you for all that you do for me, and for the agency. It was a very fortunate day when you came into the office for the first time and said that you wanted to work with me. I am very glad you did that."

"Oh, Mma," said Mma Makutsi. "I am the one who should be grateful to you. And I am—I am grateful here, Mma. I am grateful right here." She placed a hand across her heart. "Meeting you was the best thing that ever happened to me in my life." That was saying a lot. She might have given that accolade to her enrolment at the Botswana Secretarial College, but she did not. That was a close second, but meeting Mma Ramotswe was undoubtedly first.

They lapsed into silence. There were times when all that needed to be said had been said, and silence was all that remained.

CHAPTER FOURTEEN

EVERYBODY LIKES LOOKING AT CATTLE

It was in conversation with Phuti over dinner that evening that Mma Makutsi was persuaded she should tell Mma Ramotswe about her rather alarming conversation with Charlie. She had intended to keep it from her, at least until she had looked into it further, as she did not want to alarm Mma Ramotswe unnecessarily. But Phuti had taken her reports of Charlie's warning very seriously, and said that in his view Mma Ramotswe should be informed. "You cannot keep important things from people," he said. "We all have a right to know about things that affect us. It is very important—especially if steps have to be taken to protect somebody from something."

"I suppose you're right," said Mma Makutsi.

"I am definitely right," said Phuti. "And I can give you an example, Mma. We had some problems with some chairs we sold to the city council for their meeting room. There was a structural problem."

Mma Makutsi frowned. "Not enough legs?"

Phuti looked disapproving. "No, it is not funny, Grace. The chairs all had four legs, but they were not strong enough, and there were one or two cases of them giving way when important people sat on them."

Mma Makutsi made an attempt to look grave. This was difficult, as the thought of an important person sitting on a chair that then gave way had some comic possibilities—as long as the important person was not hurt, of course. It was a childish thought, but we all had a childish streak in us, buried deep beneath adult seriousness.

"I only found out about it later," continued Phuti. "One of my managers had kept it from me because he did not want me to be upset. He solved it, of course—he recalled the chairs and had one of our carpenters strengthen them, but I should have been told about it."

"Of course you should have, Phuti. That was quite wrong."

"And so I think you should tell Mma Ramotswe about what Charlie said."

Mma Makutsi agreed that she would, and the following morning when Mma Ramotswe arrived in the office, and the first pot of tea had been brewed, she raised the matter directly—perhaps rather too directly, as she began by saying, "Mma Ramotswe, I believe that Mr. J.L.B. Matekoni's life may be in danger."

Mma Ramotswe appeared not to have heard what was being said. "Oh yes, Mma," she said evenly, as if acknowledging some innocent remark about the weather. "That is very interesting . . ."

And then she stopped. "What did you say, Mma?" she asked.

Mma Makutsi repeated, "I believe that Mr. J.L.B. Matekoni's life may be in danger."

Mma Ramotswe's eyes widened. "In danger, Mma? Did you say *in danger?*"

Mma Makutsi spoke slowly. "That is what I said, Mma."

"But—"

Mma Makutsi rose to deal with the kettle, which was hissing

steam. "I will make you some tea, Mma Ramotswe. Then I shall explain."

She poured tea for Mma Ramotswe—red bush in her case, ordinary tea for herself. Then, delivering Mma Ramotswe's cup, she perched on the side of her colleague's desk as she delivered her disquieting message. "I heard this from Charlie," she began. "Charlie knows somebody who works for Mogorosi . . ."

Mma Ramotswe gasped. "Mogorosi is threatening Mr. J.L.B. Matekoni? Is that what you're saying, Mma Makutsi?"

"I'm not exactly saying that myself, Mma . . . Sometimes the things we say are the things that other people have said first, if you see what I mean, Mma." She waved a hand in the air in an attempt to convey the circulation of ideas. "Well, I suppose I am saying that, but I am just repeating what Charlie said."

"But you believe him?" asked Mma Ramotswe. "You know how Charlie can be a bit . . . imaginative." There had been a day when Mma Makutsi would have discounted everything that Charlie said; that was clearly no longer the case, and rightly so, in Mma Ramotswe's opinion, but surely some degree of caution was required.

"I know that," said Mma Makutsi. "But I think he is being quite serious about this. He spoke to a young man—some friend of his, apparently—who works for Mogorosi. This young man, who has a very large nose, apparently—"

"What has that got to do with it, Mma?" asked Mma Ramotswe.

"Nothing, really. It is just a bit of background information. Anyway, this friend of Charlie's is Mogorosi's driver, and he had heard that his boss and Mr. J.L.B. Matekoni were seeing more of one another, and he thought that he should warn Charlie that Mr. J.L.B. Matekoni should be very careful about where he walked. Those were the words he used, apparently: *he should be very careful about where he walked.*

Mma Ramotswe sat back in her chair. Her cup of tea was left untouched on the desk in front of her. "But why?" she asked. "Why should Mogorosi want to harm his friend? Have they fallen out?"

Mma Makutsi shook her head. "No, they haven't. But to tell you the truth, Mma, I have been suspicious of that man ever since he suddenly turned up here. I thought, What does this man want from Mr. J.L.B. Matekoni? That is what I thought. The words in my mind were *Oh yes?* When you think *Oh yes*, then you have to pay attention. There is always a reason why you should say to yourself *Oh yes*."

Mma Ramotswe looked thoughtful. "I know what you mean, Mma. It seemed a rather sudden friendship. But I still cannot see why Mogorosi should want to harm Mr. J.L.B. Matekoni. That is quite different."

Mma Makutsi explained that while she agreed that it seemed unlikely, Charlie had suggested a good reason why Mogorosi might want Mr. J.L.B. Matekoni out of the way. She explained it while Mma Ramotswe drank her tea, her expression one of close attention. When she finished, Mma Makutsi looked enquiringly at Mma Ramotswe. "What do you think, Mma?" she asked. "It could be, couldn't it?"

Mma Ramotswe took a little time to answer. Then at last she said, "I have had dreams about that crocodile, you know."

Mma Makutsi waited.

At length, Mma Ramotswe said, "I know that it was Mogorosi in the water, and not Mr. J.L.B. Matekoni. I know that. But I have had two dreams—bad dreams, Mma—in which it was the other way round. And I have woken up feeling very sad that my husband has been eaten, and fortunately, there he is beside me. It is not pleasant, Mma Makutsi."

"Well—" began Mma Makutsi.

Mma Ramotswe did not let her finish. "I take this very seriously, Mma. But what do we do? If I go to Mr. J.L.B. Matekoni and tell him about what Charlie has said, I think he will say that everybody is imagining things."

"True."

"So perhaps we should deal with this ourselves," Mma Ramotswe went on. "We may have to tell him about it, but not just yet."

Mma Makutsi agreed. "Charlie says that we can speak to this friend of his," she said. "I think we should do that, Mma. We may find out more about what the exact danger is."

She returned to her own desk and they finished their tea in silence, each lost in the contemplation of this entirely unexpected and distressing development. In all her years as a private detective, Mma Ramotswe had never felt what she now felt: a real sense of dread. Botswana was a peaceful country—this sort of thing happened elsewhere, but it was not how people conducted themselves in Gaborone. And yet, could anywhere—even this quiet, well-behaved country—be immune to the undercurrent of threat and insecurity that seemed to be so much an entrenched feature of the modern world? It seemed it could not. Sooner or later somebody like Mogorosi, an unlikely villain perhaps, would bring to their lives a reminder of the unpleasantness that human nature was capable of demonstrating—even in the best-regulated society.

Mma Ramotswe sighed. "We should go and speak to this friend of Charlie's as soon as possible. Can you call Charlie in, Mma Makutsi?"

Mma Makutsi left the office to find Charlie, who was working in the garage. She returned a few minutes later, with Charlie in tow.

"She's told you, Mma?" enquired Charlie, wiping his hands on the sides of his overalls.

"She has," said Mma Ramotswe.

Charlie shook his head. "Bad news, Mma. I never liked that man. And if he got hold of this place, you could imagine what would happen to all of us. History—we'd be history, Mma. Gone."

Mma Makutsi gasped. "But what about Mr. J.L.B. Matekoni? What happens to the garage is nothing beside the issue of what happens to Mr. J.L.B. Matekoni."

Charlie was quick to reassure her that Mr. J.L.B. Matekoni's safety was more important than anything else. "I care about the boss," he said. "That's what we all care about."

Mma Makutsi frowned. "Where is he, by the way?"

They both looked at Mma Ramotswe. "He said something about taking his truck to collect a car. He should be back soon."

Charlie looked puzzled. "His truck is still there." He went to the door and glanced outside. "Yes, it's there. It hasn't been moved since he arrived this morning."

"So where is he?" asked Mma Makutsi.

Charlie shrugged. Then he seemed to recollect something. "He did say something about going somewhere. I didn't pay much attention, I'm afraid. I was under a car."

Mma Makutsi glowered. "You can't remember what he said?"

Charlie looked defensive. "I can't remember everything that everybody says, Mma. Fanwell is always talking about something or other—*ya, ya, ya*—and I can't be expected to make notes."

"Where is Fanwell?" asked Mma Ramotswe.

"He's got three days off. His uncle up in Francistown has become late. They are having a big funeral up there. Fanwell's cousins have come all the way from Mozambique. There are lots of his people there. They will all be up there, eating and drinking. Fanwell says his cousins are very greedy." Charlie paused. "I think Fanwell can be greedy too, you know. It's genetic, maybe. Fatso father, fatso son. Same same."

Mma Makutsi interrupted him. "Fanwell is not overweight, Charlie. If anything, he's a bit thin. And you don't call people fatso these days."

"Even if they are?" asked Charlie.

Mma Makutsi pursed her lips with disapproval.

"He ate three fat cakes the other day," Charlie continued. "I saw him—I swear, I saw him. Three—"

"This is not about fat cakes," Mma Makutsi scolded. "This is about where Mr. J.L.B. Matekoni has got to."

Charlie held up his hands in mock defence. "Sorry. My fault. As always. Charlie's fault. Charlie's fault. Want to blame somebody? Blame Charlie. You asked me—"

Mma Ramotswe made a calming gesture. These spats between Mma Makutsi and Charlie blew up less often than they used to, but they could still occur. "Let's not argue. What I want to find out is where Mr. J.L.B. Matekoni is."

Charlie suddenly looked worried. "You don't think he's with Mogorosi, do you, Mma? Did he say anything about seeing him?"

Mma Ramotswe said that she could not recall his saying anything about meeting his friend, but the fact that his truck was still where he had parked it suggested that he had been picked up by somebody. It could well have been Mogorosi.

Charlie had an idea. "I could call Big Nose. He'll know where Mogorosi is. He's his driver."

"Call him now," said Mma Makutsi.

"If he's getting reception," said Charlie. "But I could try."

"Then please do it," said Mma Makutsi.

Charlie went outside to make the call. While he was outside, Mma Makutsi made an effort to reassure Mma Ramotswe. "He'll turn up in town somewhere, Mma. Somebody might have brought a car for him to look at—that sort of thing. You mustn't worry."

"I shall try," said Mma Ramotswe. "He usually tells me when—"

She did not finish. Charlie came back in to face the expectant stares of the two women. He stood in the doorway and spoke—a messenger with an unwelcome message. "Mogorosi has a cattle post not all that far from town," he said. "Fifteen miles."

"And?" pressed Mma Makutsi.

"He's driving out there now. He said that Mogorosi took his own vehicle out first, but wanted his car brought out by Big Nose."

"And?" Mma Makutsi repeated.

"The boss was with Mogorosi. They were going out there together."

There was silence as they digested this.

"Why?" asked Mma Ramotswe.

Charlie did not know. "Maybe to look at cattle. Mogorosi has some fine cattle. The boss likes looking at cattle, I think." He paused. "Everybody likes looking at cattle, and the boss is only human—just like the rest of us." He was insouciant, but it was hard, and the façade slipped. In his concern, he was unable to stop a small groan. "The boss . . ."

Mma Ramotswe rose from her chair. This was the No. 1 Ladies' Detective Agency, and she was in charge. This was her husband they were talking about. "Do you know where this place is, Charlie?" she asked.

"I've never been there," Charlie replied. "But Big Nose told me about it once. There's a country store out there. I know the son of the man who owns that. I know where that is."

Mma Ramotswe spoke decisively. "We'll all go," she said.

She tried to keep calm. This was in all likelihood an entirely innocent trip into the country. People liked any excuse to go to their cattle posts, and Mogorosi would be no exception. He would be proud of his cattle and would enjoy showing them to his new friend. That must be the explanation. But at the same time a major doubt had taken root in her mind, and it was the sort of anxiety that would not easily go away.

CHAPTER FIFTEEN

THE SMELL OF DISINFECTANT

THEY TOOK MMA MAKUTSI'S CAR, which was considerably larger than Mma Ramotswe's van, and therefore more comfortable. It also had air conditioning, and even if that currently did not work—Charlie said it was something to do with fluid levels—its presence was comforting. "The most reliable form of air conditioning," Mma Makutsi remarked, "is an open window."

Since he knew the way, Mma Makutsi suggested that Charlie should drive, while she and Mma Ramotswe occupied the rear seats, where they could talk about agency matters. In the event, Mma Ramotswe was in no mood for such conversation, her mind being preoccupied with thoughts of the possible danger that Mr. J.L.B. Matekoni was now facing—if Charlie was to be believed. She suspected that her fears were probably groundless, but that was not enough to stop her from picturing him being trussed up and abandoned in the bush somewhere while a heartless Mogorosi made good his escape. Botswana was so large and so much of it was so empty that anyone abandoned in the wild would be very difficult to locate in time to be saved. Thirst was the great enemy, of course, but there were others, including predators. There were hyenas and leopards, and even lions if one went far enough into the Kalahari. And snakes, too, including the aggressive black mamba, said to be fast enough to overtake a galloping horse, and a bite from which could cause agonising death within minutes. There was so much to worry about . . .

Mma Makutsi did her best to take Mma Ramotswe's mind off what she rightly assumed to be morbid imaginings. She spoke about Phuti and his recent trip to a trade fair over the border, where he had been introduced to the latest lines in chairs—none of which, he claimed, could be sat in with any degree of comfort.

"Modern people must be designed differently," he complained to Mma Makutsi. "These chairs look good, but are the wrong shape for most people, I think. Perhaps very fashionable people fit in them—perhaps such people are all sharp angles and so on and so on."

Mma Ramotswe listened, but with only half an ear. Phuti was right about modern chairs: in her view, most of them were far too small to be comfortable in. They were chairs to keep you on your toes, and awake even when you were hoping to enjoy a few snatched moments of sleep.

"And Phuti says the same is true of beds these days," Mma Makutsi went on. "It is all very well for small people, but for those who are more generously proportioned, if they turn round in their sleep, they wake up on the floor. Phuti says this is very serious. One of his customers has had to buy two beds in order to get a good night's sleep."

"Oh yes . . ."

And so the largely one-sided conversation continued until Charlie turned off the public road onto a side-track leading off through acacia scrub. "I can see that vehicles have been along here recently," he commented over his shoulder. "See the tracks? That will be Mogorosi and then Big Nose. Two vehicles. Right there."

Mma Makutsi urged him to hurry, but Charlie resisted. "You go too fast, Mma, and what happens? Broken suspension—that's what. And then we're in trouble."

They travelled on in silence. Here and there, a short way off the track, were signs of local habitation—a hut constructed of brushwood and daub, the occasional stock enclosure—a circle of rough wooden posts—a path littered with the droppings of goats. It was hard country, although the recent fall of rain had touched it with green. There were birds—a mocking lourie, the go-away bird, with its insistent, discouraging call; the ubiquitous Cape doves; a small flock of glossy starlings. And they felt the eyes of cattle upon them, although there were none to be seen. The cattle would be there, dark shapes in the olive green of the acacia bush, patient and quietly getting on with their grazing, in the way of all cattle.

And then, suddenly, they were on the edge of an area of cleared land, in the centre of which were two small tin-roofed buildings constructed of grey breeze-blocks. To the side of one of these, a pickup truck and a white car were parked under such shade as was provided by a small thorn tree.

Charlie turned to address his passengers. "Hah, you see, ladies? Everything's fine. That's Mogorosi's pickup and his car. Both there."

Mma Ramotswe's gaze moved across the scene. It was a typical cattle post, of a sort that one might find anywhere in Botswana, and it brought back memories of going to such places when she was a girl. Her father often took her with him when he went to see his cattle, and she would cook for him on an open fire, and at night there would be field upon field of stars and the sound that the stars seemed to make in the darkness, which of course was not the sound of stars at all but that of the insects calling to one another from their hidden places.

"But where are they?" she asked Charlie, as he stopped the engine.

Charlie looked about him. "They will be nearby, Mma. They will be with the cattle."

Mma Makutsi frowned. "What are we going to say?" she asked. "They will ask why we are here, I think."

Charlie looked at Mma Ramotswe. "That's a good point," he said. "We can hardly say that we've come because we think that Mogorosi is planning to harm Mr. J.L.B. Matekoni."

"We will think of something," said Mma Ramotswe. "We might say—"

She did not finish. From the other side of the clearing, from beyond the two small buildings, there came a cry. Then another one—a shout, more urgent this time.

Mma Ramotswe struggled to make out what was happening. Figures had appeared from the side of one of the buildings, and she saw at a glance that there were four of them—one a boy. She recognised Mr. J.L.B. Matekoni, and she felt a surge of relief, but then the figures moved about and she saw that one of them had dropped to the ground. Another stooped, and yet another seemed to detach himself from the group and came running towards them, only to turn back almost immediately. She gasped, and reached for Mma Makutsi's arm, and gripped it tightly in her fright and her misery. They were too late—whatever it was that they had feared was going to happen was being enacted there before them, under the full glare of the morning sun.

Charlie was soon out of the car, leaving the driver's door open behind him, running across the patch of ground that separated them from the group of people. Now Mma Makutsi opened her door, and the women were somehow outside, following Charlie in his dash. There was a young man, and she realised it was Big Nose. He was shouting something to Charlie, who brushed past him to the place where the two men, and the boy, were in a disorganised huddle on the ground.

Mma Ramotswe's only thought was of Mr. J.L.B. Matekoni. Something had clearly happened, but she was unable to think much about that: she wanted now only to be at his side. Was he on the ground, or was that someone else? Was he looking down on a collapsed figure—he was, she thought—or was that Mogorosi? In the panic and chaos of the moment, she could not tell.

But now she was upon them, and it was Mr. J.L.B. Matekoni standing, half bent down to attend to Mogorosi, who was on the ground, clutching his legs. And there was blood, just a trickle on the khaki of a trouser leg, and that sight told her everything. Mogorosi had been bitten by a snake.

Mr. J.L.B. Matekoni shouted, "There was a snake . . . a snake!"

She knelt down beside the writhing man. She took hold of his arm. "What happened, Rra?"

He tried to give an answer, but she could not make out what he was saying. She thought that perhaps he was crying. She turned and looked up at Mr. J.L.B. Matekoni. "We must get him back into town. We must go to the hospital."

"Of course."

Big Nose and Charlie had gone off to look through the door of one of the buildings. Now they returned.

"Bad news," stuttered Charlie. "A puff adder. A big one."

Mma Ramotswe drew in her breath. A puff adder bite was particularly serious if a large amount of venom had been injected. Big snakes had more venom, and longer fangs. If the snake that bit Mogorosi had been able to get a good grip, it would have done a great deal of damage.

Mma Makutsi and Mr. J.L.B. Matekoni now helped Mogorosi to his feet.

"Can you walk, Rra?" asked Mma Makutsi.

"We can carry him," said Big Nose. "I can take his legs and somebody else can take his arms. We can carry him."

Now Mogorosi spoke. "I can walk. Just give me a hand—I can walk."

On the way back, Mma Ramotswe took control. She and Mma Makutsi would accompany Mogorosi in his car, to be driven by Big Nose. The others could follow in the remaining vehicles. They would make their way, as fast as the track would permit, back to the main road, and then they would be only half an hour or so from the Princess Marina Hospital. If the traffic was light, they might be there even quicker.

It did not take long to get Mogorosi into the back seat of his car. Mma Makutsi and Mma Ramotswe sat on either side of him, doing their best to comfort him. As he settled himself, he gave a wince of pain. "It is as if my leg is on fire," he said. "All the way up. Fire."

"It will not be long," said Mma Ramotswe. "We will be there soon and they will give you what you need. They do this every day."

"I am going to die," said Mogorosi. His tone was matter of fact, as if he were giving voice to an intention.

"You will not die, Rra," said Mma Ramotswe. It was an instruction—not a prediction.

"I didn't see the snake," said Mogorosi. "It was in the hut."

It was the first time that any mention had been made of how the encounter with the puff adder had occurred. Mma Ramotswe hesitated; the real point now was not to establish what had happened but to save Mogorosi's life.

"These bites are very bad," muttered Mma Makutsi. "The poison destroys the tissues. That is very bad."

Mma Ramotswe gave Mma Makutsi a disapproving glance, and Mma Makutsi fell silent. But Mogorosi seemed not to have heard this discouraging prognosis. Now he said, "I should have looked. You don't go into those buildings out here without looking where you're going."

"It is easily done, Rra," said Mma Ramotswe. But what she was thinking was this: Had the snake been put there to bite Mr. J.L.B. Matekoni? Had it—like that crocodile in the dam—simply got the wrong man? Once again, it occurred to her that this was a plot that had gone wrong, and that it could so easily have been her own husband lying there in agony.

Big Nose drove in silence, and very fast. Soon they were back in the traffic of town, passing cars with their horn blaring to give warning of the emergency. And then they were turning into the grounds of the hospital and sweeping up to the shaded doors where the ambulances discharged their casualties. From that point, everything happened rather quickly. Mogorosi was placed on a trolley and whisked off down a corridor, attended by a doctor in a loose blue uniform. Mma Ramotswe and Mma Makutsi found chairs in a niche off the corridor, and sat down; Big Nose muttered something about joining Mr. J.L.B. Matekoni and Charlie, who had gone off to find Mma Mogorosi, who needed to be told about her husband.

After an hour or so, a nurse came to speak to Mma Ramotswe and Mma Makutsi. "Who is the wife?" she asked.

"We are his friends," said Mma Makutsi. "We are not married to him. We brought him in."

The nurse nodded. "You can see him now, if you like. Maybe just one of you, as he is still recovering."

Mma Makutsi turned to Mma Ramotswe. "You go, Mma. I do not like hospital wards very much. You go, and I'll wait."

Mma Ramotswe left Mma Makutsi and followed the nurse down the corridor. There was the smell of disinfectant in the air, and that triggered memories of the school at Mochudi, on its commanding hill, looking down over the plains below. The school janitor was often seen with his tin enamelled bucket, chipped around its rim, from which he liberally dispensed this very disinfectant over the floors of the classrooms, muttering, as he did so, about germs. For a moment she was back there, a girl of ten, on one of those hot mornings. Listening to the scrape of the teacher's chalk on the blackboard. Even if there were large changes in the world, the small things often remained the same.

They entered a ward in which a dozen beds lined the walls on each side. She saw Mogorosi, lying on top of a white sheet, his leg bandaged, a tube linking his arm to a suspended bottle. He turned to look at her, and grinned weakly.

"Mma Ramotswe . . ."

She told him that he should not bother to talk. "You need to rest now, Rra. I just wanted to make sure you are all right."

"They have given me an injection," he said. "It will deal with the snake's venom. It already has made a big difference."

"You look better, I think."

"I am much better."

She stared at him. There was so much that she wanted to ask him, but she was not sure how she could say any of it. But she did not need to speak.

"I wanted to talk to you," he said. He made a gesture with his hand that suggested there was a lot to discuss. She wondered what he would have to say. Perhaps there might be a confession, now that his second attempt on the life of Mr. J.L.B. Matekoni had failed. How could anybody be so evil, she asked herself—if any of this was true. But it had to be; it would be too much of a coincidence for Mr. J.L.B. Matekoni to be so close to danger in incidents that were just days apart. It was just so unlikely.

She sat down on the chair beside his bed. "I am listening, Rra," she said.

He looked at her with what appeared to be gratitude. "My life has been saved twice now. First, when I was almost taken by a crocodile—you heard about that, Mma?"

"I did."

"And that was by my friend Mr. J.L.B. Matekoni. He is a brave man, Mma—your husband is a brave man, you know."

She waited.

"And then by you and that other lady—"

"Mma Makutsi."

"Yes. Her. You brought me to this place, where the doctors saved my life again." He paused. "How many times can a man's life be saved, Mma? Do you know the answer to that?"

She shrugged. "Many times, I think, Rra. It all depends."

He nodded, as if a perfectly satisfactory answer had been given.

Then he said something that made Mma Ramotswe blink with surprise.

"And how many mistakes can a man make before he realises he's made too many, Mma?"

He looked at her through half-closed eyes—was he still in pain, she wondered; or was that the effect of painkillers?

He did not wait for her to answer. "I have made too many in my lifetime, Mma."

She held his gaze. "We all make mistakes, Rra. All of us."

He nodded. "And sometimes we do things that are worse than mistakes," he continued.

She lowered her eyes. She had not expected a confession—not

so quickly—but sometimes people felt a pressing need to unburden themselves and could not wait. Was this such a situation? She raised her eyes again and gave Mogorosi an appraising look. Did he look contrite? Possibly—it was difficult to tell.

"I have done Mr. J.L.B. Matekoni a great wrong," said Mogorosi. "A very great wrong."

Mma Ramotswe was silent. He was right: it was difficult to imagine a greater wrong than trying to arrange for somebody to be eaten by a crocodile or, indeed, to be bitten by a puff adder.

She decided to make it easier for him. "You must feel very troubled, Rra. If you plan to kill somebody, you are in a very dark place—"

She did not finish.

"Kill somebody, Mma? Who was planning to kill anybody?"

She frowned. "Mr. J.L.B. Matekoni," she said. "The crocodile . . ."

Mogorosi gasped. "Mr. J.L.B. Matekoni was planning to kill me? He wouldn't even kill a fly, Mma." He raised a hand in protest, weakly, and then dropped it. "No, Mma, nobody has been planning to kill anybody. The only person planning to do anything like that was the crocodile! And it almost got *me*."

"And that snake . . ."

He gave her an anguished look. "That snake had nothing to do with anything. It just happened to be there."

She looked thoughtful. There was no doubt in her mind now that he was telling the truth. "What was the great wrong you were talking about, Rra?"

He lay back in his bed. "I was going to take advantage of him, Mma. I had nominated him for membership of a board. I did that because I wanted to have somebody who would approve of some applications I was going to make. If I was on the board myself, I would not have been able to vote on my own case. I wanted a friend there instead—a good friend." He paused. "Somebody like

Mr. J.L.B. Matekoni, who would vote in my favour when I made my application to purchase new businesses."

It did not take Mma Ramotswe long to work out what had happened: after what Mogorosi had said, it seemed only too obvious.

"And then," Mogorosi went on, "and then Mr. J.L.B. Matekoni saved my life when I fell out of the boat. And I thought, How can I treat the man who saved my life in this way? I am not a wicked man, Mma, but I could not use a man like that."

"No," mused Mma Ramotswe. "I don't imagine you could."

"I was going to talk to him," Mogorosi went on. "I was going to tell him what I had done and I was going to ask for his forgiveness. Maybe he wouldn't be able to forgive me—I would not be surprised if that were so, but I would still ask him. I think that—"

Mma Ramotswe stopped him. "I can tell you one thing, Rra. Mr. J.L.B. Matekoni would forgive you. I know him—he is my husband—and I know that he would never refuse to forgive somebody who was truly sorry."

"But that's me," said Mogorosi. "I am truly sorry, Mma. I am that man."

"Then you will find that you are forgiven, Rra. You talk to him and tell him what you have told me, and you will hear him forgive you. That is definite, Rra—no question about it."

Mogorosi stared at her. "Are you sure, Mma Ramotswe?"

"Oh, I am sure, Rra. You will be forgiven."

"Then I am a very fortunate man," he said. "And I have found a good friend at last. Mr. J.L.B. Matekoni . . . and you, of course, Mma. Double good fortune for me."

Mma Ramotswe bit her lip. She had her reservations about Mogorosi's friendship with Mr. J.L.B. Matekoni being continued—after all that had happened—but then she remembered about not being able to choose one's husband's friends. An imperfect friend, she told herself, was better than no friend at all. Possibly. She would have to think about that, though; perhaps Mma Potokwane might have views on this. She would raise it with her when next they met, and she would see what Mma Potokwane had to say on the matter. Over a cup of tea, of course, and a slice . . . well, two slices, perhaps, of fruit cake.

CHAPTER SIXTEEN

PEOPLE CAN BE HARD ON MEN

MMA POTOKWANE had been expecting her friend, she said, although she had had no idea when Mma Ramotswe's tiny white van would make its dusty way up the road to the Orphan Farm at Tlokweng. "I felt that you were coming to see me, Mma Ramotswe," she said. "You know how you can feel that something is going to happen, although you are not sure when it will happen? And then, ninety-nine times out of a hundred, it happens, and you think, I knew that was going to happen."

"I know that feeling well, Mma," said Mma Ramotswe. "I get it sometimes when Mma Makutsi is about to say something. I think, Now Mma Makutsi is going to say something about the Botswana Secretarial College and, the next moment, she says it. It is very strange."

Mma Potokwane looked thoughtful. "I'm not sure it's *that* strange, Mma Ramotswe. People tend to say the same things, you know. And yes, I have heard Mma Makutsi mentioning the Botswana Secretarial College more than once. She is very proud of it, I think."

"With good reason," said Mma Ramotswe, remembering the effort it must have cost Mma Makutsi's family to send her to the college all the way from Bobonong to Gaborone. The fees were always kept as low as possible, she believed, but they would have been a large slice out of the income of a family that would have had many other claims on its meagre resources. But they had risen to the occasion—uncles, aunts, and even remoter relatives—and Mma Makutsi had made the best possible use of the opportunity, as people often did when they had to scrimp and save to achieve their goal. Yes, Mma Makutsi did not hesitate to express her pride, but it was a justifiable pride and Mma Ramotswe would never think the less of her for that.

And if she thought of her own life, she, too, could feel a certain measure of satisfaction with what she had achieved. Mma Ramotswe had not had the advantage of an education that went beyond a few years of high school, but that had not stopped her. To start her business, she had used the funds from the sale of many of the cattle she inherited from her late daddy, that great, good man, Obed Ramotswe, proud citizen of Botswana. Not a day went past that she didn't think of him, and of his gentleness and goodness, which was typical of the men of his generation. It was so unfair: people elsewhere sometimes judged Africa harshly—they needed to think more about men like her father, who was composed almost entirely of goodness and kindness; who always thought of others who were needier than he was; and who was still there, in a sense, in the same way as a fond memory will stay with one long after others are relegated to oblivion. *Late people are still with us . . .* yes, they were. Obed Ramotswe was still there, a presence in her life, mostly silent, in the nature of things, as the voices of the late people were like the softest whispers of the wind, detectable only if one really wanted to hear them. He was there—she was sure of it, in those places that those who know Botswana will recognise, in those skies that you may think are empty, in the echoes that return from the small hills of red rock, in the look that you glimpsed in the eyes of the sweet-breathed cattle.

All the ancestors were there, in such things, if you were prepared to see them.

But now she was approaching the gates of the Orphan Farm, and she could see the tops of the trees that surrounded Mma Potokwane's office—eucalyptus trees that had shot up, as such trees do when given the slightest encouragement. And, as she turned off the public road, the tiny white van seemed to find its own way among the bumps and indentations in the untarred road, as if it had its own memory. Of course, Mr. J.L.B. Matekoni would have said that it did—he had always maintained that steering would find the most comfortable way if you pointed it in roughly the right direction. "Never over-steer," he said. "There are people who turn the steering wheel this way and that all the time—that only confuses a vehicle. Most cars know the way home, you know—and all we have to do is to give them the smallest amount of help."

Mma Potokwane came out to meet her, embracing her in the way of an old friend, which was what she was—Mma Ramotswe's oldest friend, perhaps.

"We could go for a walk, Mma Ramotswe," suggested Mma Potokwane. "I have been sitting in my office all day and I need to stretch my legs."

Mma Ramotswe was happy to agree, and they set off in the direction of the playing field where the children played their games of football. A few of the boys were kicking a ball around, aiming at improvised goalposts, shouting at the tops of their voices.

"Children love shouting," said Mma Potokwane. "I think I have spoken to you before about that. I may have told you that noise levels are the sign. You don't need a thermometer to tell you if a child is unwell. You just listen for the noise—or for the silence. If a child stops shouting, there is something wrong, I've always thought."

"And adults?" asked Mma Ramotswe. "Do we not like to shout?"

"Not so much," said Mma Potokwane. "Although perhaps we should, Mma. Perhaps we should occasionally stand still and open up our lungs and shout. Perhaps we would feel better if we did that."

The boys waved, and Mma Potokwane waved back. "One of those is that boy you met," said Mma Potokwane. "You remember him, Mma? I told you about him." She paused. As matron of the Orphan Farm, she had developed the ability to remember details. She remembered what had happened in the young lives of those in her care—all the setbacks, the tragedies large and small that had brought children to this particular door. But that was her job—and she knew that although others might hear these stories, and be moved by them, they might not always remember them. Or they might fade, one into the other, as tales of the world's misfortunes tended to do. There was just too much; there was just too much pain in the world for people to remember the ins and outs of how suffering came to be.

She thought that she would jog Mma Ramotswe's memory. "He is called Thabiso. Remember? You spoke to him, Mma. He is a very polite little boy."

Mma Ramotswe was gazing at the dusty football pitch. Any grass that might have had the courage to show itself after the recent rains would have given up under the onslaught of these exuberant players. No matter: all that was required was a ball and a bit of room in which to kick it about. And there was plenty of room in Botswana; there was still enough room in this world for us to live out our lives, and yet there were so many people who wanted to stop others from doing it.

"Thabiso?" said Mma Ramotswe. "I remember him. Of course I remember him, Mma Potokwane."

Mma Potokwane smiled. "You gave him a prize. I think you might have wanted to do it without anybody else knowing. But I hear everything that goes on round here, Mma. Everything."

Mma Ramotswe laughed. "I have never doubted that, Mma. I

hear you have many spies. Throughout the country. People talk about Mma Potokwane's intelligence service. I think they call it that. They say your people are better even than the government's intelligence service."

It was Mma Potokwane's turn to laugh. "That is very interesting, Mma. I have not heard that from any of my agents. They must be sleeping too much."

They both watched the boys. The game was entering a particularly exciting phase. A goal was about to be scored, and then it was—to the delight of one side and the overacted disappointment of the other. Mma Potokwane clapped her hands together to attract the children's attention. "Thabiso!" she called out. "Thabiso, come over here, please."

There was a small boy who had been on the side that had scored the goal. He had turned a cartwheel in his excitement—and they had witnessed it. Now, he detached himself and ran obediently across the pitch to where the two women were standing. Coming to a halt, he squinted up first at Mma Potokwane, and then at Mma Ramotswe, uttering the polite, traditional greeting.

"So, Thabiso," said Mma Potokwane. "Your side has scored a goal. Was it a big goal then?"

The boy broke into a smile. "A very big goal, Mma. Just like the Zebras."

The Zebras were the national team, and everybody approved of them.

"The Zebras!" exclaimed Mma Potokwane. "They will be watching you boys. They will be thinking, Which one should we pick to come and play with us? Perhaps there is a boy called Thabiso—we have heard that he is a first-class player. Perhaps he will come and play with us at the stadium sometime soon. Maybe when he has his eighth birthday."

Thabiso's eyes widened. "That would be very good, Mma. I would go straightaway—if they asked me. I am ready."

Mma Potokwane and Mma Ramotswe shared an amused glance. Then Mma Potokwane continued, "You remember this lady, Thabiso. I think you will remember who she is."

The boy transferred his gaze to Mma Ramotswe. He lowered his eyes in respect. A child should not stare too long at an adult, according to the old ways. "I remember her, Mma. This is the lady who gave me a prize."

Mma Potokwane was pleased. "Yes, that is right, Thabiso," she said. "This is that kind lady."

Mma Ramotswe reached out to take his hand. It was moist from exertion. She gave it a squeeze. "And I remember you, Thabiso. I remember thinking, This boy is very good at sports. That is what I thought. And I thought, too, This boy will be a big strong man quite soon. If he eats all his food he will grow big and strong."

"I am doing that, Mma. I am eating all my food."

Mma Ramotswe smiled. "That is good." And yes, it was good, when you were a growing boy, but the rest of us should be careful; fat cakes are a temptation to which we should not always give in. To show weakness on occasion was permissible, but this should not be done too often. Willpower was the issue, she thought, and one day, she decided, she would do something about getting more of it. But not just yet . . .

"Actually, Mma Ramotswe," said Mma Potokwane, "Thabiso has something for you." She smiled at the boy. "Isn't that so, Thabiso?"

The boy nodded his head gravely. "Yes, Mma," he said. "I have something."

"Then run along and fetch it," Mma Potokwane instructed him.

The boy turned on his heel and ran off towards a small building—one of the children's houses. They watched him as he made his way.

"He can run, that boy," said Mma Potokwane. "He will be a very good sportsman." She sighed. "The mother has stopped being in touch. You may remember, I told you that she was a bar lady—which is putting it politely."

Mma Ramotswe remembered. "And the father, you said, was in prison."

"Yes," said Mma Potokwane. "We were hoping that we might be able to reintegrate Thabiso into his family, but it's too far gone for that. The mother is no good. That's all there is to it."

Mma Ramotswe looked up at the sky. She never liked to write anybody off, but she had to agree with Mma Potokwane, even if reluctantly: there were some people who would never make anything of their lives, no matter what help they were given. These people inevitably caused disappointment after disappointment. Perhaps Thabiso's mother was like that—it sounded as if she was. She closed her eyes. Were there circumstances in which one just had to give up and accept that nothing could be done? She had been brought up by her father never to give up hope. That was the right approach, she felt, but there came a point when there was no more to be done.

"He's coming back," observed Mma Potokwane.

Mma Ramotswe opened her eyes to see the small figure of Thabiso returning across the playing field. In a short time he was with them, his hands behind his back, concealing something.

"You can give it to Mma Ramotswe," encouraged Mma Potokwane. "Don't be shy."

The boy hesitated, and then held out his hands, one cupped over the other. After a moment or two he removed the top hand to reveal a small wooden carving of a bird. "It is for you, Mma," he said, handing it to Mma Ramotswe.

She took the bird from him and held it up to examine it. It was a hornbill, a familiar resident of the Botswana bush, distinguished by its out-of-proportion, curved yellow bill and its large eyes. How many times had she been observed by these birds, with their wise-old-man look, from a branch of an acacia tree or a fencepost. How many times when she had been walking had she been disturbed by the flight of one of these birds from a place of concealment off in the direction of another perch. They were one of the most common birds, but at the same time one of the strangest in appearance.

Mma Ramotswe looked down on Thabiso. "This is very kind," she said. "Are you sure this is for me?"

The boy nodded gravely. "I made it for you, Mma. It is a present for you."

She struggled to speak. This small boy, who had so little, whose young life had got off to such a difficult start, must have spent hours carving this for her.

She held it up against the sky. She noticed the detail. She said to Mma Potokwane, "Look, Mma. See how perfect it is."

Mma Potokwane inclined her head. "Perfect, Mma."

"I wouldn't be surprised if it spread its wings and started to fly," said Mma Ramotswe.

Thabiso said gravely, "It cannot fly, Mma."

He shifted from foot to foot. He glanced over his shoulder to where his friends were still playing football.

"You had better get back to the others," said Mma Potokwane. "Without you, your team will never be able to win the match, will it?"

He grinned, and turned to run off. Mma Ramotswe held the small carving to her breast. She struggled with her tears, but it was an unequal battle. Mma Potokwane understood. She reached out and put a hand on her friend's shoulder. "I know, Mma," she whispered. "I know how it is."

They stood still for a few further moments. Then, by unspoken consent, they abandoned their walk and began to make their way back to the office.

"I sometimes think it will get easier as time goes by," Mma Potokwane said. "But it doesn't, you know."

"No?"

"No. I think sometimes that I have shed all the tears that can be shed, but then I find that this is simply not true."

"No?"

"No."

THEY SETTLED DOWN to the tea that Mma Potokwane had prepared in her office. There was a freshly baked fruit cake, pristine and uncut in its perfect circle. Soon a large wedge, forty-five degrees or more, had been cut and handed to Mma Ramotswe on a plate. A large cup of red bush tea followed, while Mma Potokwane poured her own cup of Five Roses.

To begin with their conversation was general. There was talk about the rains, because that was what everybody talked about at the start of the rainy season. But there was a limit to what could be said about rain and its effect on the land, and so this was followed by a short silence, as they tackled their fruit cake and tea. Then, at exactly the same time, as if orchestrated by some hidden conductor, they both said, "Modise—"

They stopped and looked at one another in astonishment.

"I was—" Again, they both uttered the same words at exactly the same time.

Now, laughter was the only possible response, before Mma Potokwane, as host, made a graceful gesture of her hand—an invitation for Mma Ramotswe to speak.

"I was going to tell you, Mma Potokwane," she began. "I was going to tell you—and I can see that you were thinking exactly the same thing . . ."

"About Mr. Excellence Modise?"

"Yes. About him."

Mma Potokwane indicated that she was keen to hear more. "I had been wondering, Mma Ramotswe. I had been thinking."

"You had been thinking, Mma?"

Mma Potokwane sat back in her chair, wiping as she did so a few crumbs of fruit cake from her lower lip. She had often noticed that as one went through life, one effect of the passage of years was a tendency for crumbs and other such things to congregate on one's lips, or, in the case of liquids, to leave their appointed limits and occasionally dribble down the chin. It was, people said, an inevitable consequence of growing slightly older—not that she, or Mma Ramotswe, were getting on unduly. They were forty-something, or thereabouts—and although that was not exactly the first flush of youth, it was not yet time to start sitting in the sun and watching the cattle graze. And yet there was no doubt that age—or perhaps, one might say, the growth of wisdom—had an effect on the structure of the lower lip and the chin. It was an interesting subject, and one that might at a more appropriate time be the subject of frank discussion—but not now.

"I was thinking about that man," Mma Potokwane continued. "And I was wondering whether your investigations had led to any conclusions." She paused. There was a note of apology in her voice, which puzzled Mma Ramotswe.

"There have been developments," said Mma Ramotswe.

She was about to expand on this, but Mma Potokwane took over. "You see, Mma, I realise that I was too hard on that man. When we discussed him, I was a bit . . . how shall I put it, Mma? I was a bit uncharitable."

Mma Ramotswe recalled exactly what Mma Potokwane had said. It had been clear that she had no time for Excellence—which was very much how she herself had felt then.

"And I think I have reached a different conclusion now," said Mma Potokwane. "I have worked out what happened—or what I think is likely to have been going on."

Mma Ramotswe raised an eyebrow.

"I think that when he came to see you about his wife, he was not lying—as I suggested. I called him a liar, Mma Ramotswe. I said to you—that man will be lying. Do you remember that?"

Mma Ramotswe nodded. "I believe that is what you said, Mma."

"Well, I think now that I was wrong. I think that Modise was telling the truth. I think that his wife was probably having an affair. I think that she will come to you and say that she thinks he is seeing somebody. I think that she will then set things up so that you think that he is having an affair, when he really only wants to get back with his wife. I think she might even arrange for some woman to tempt him into an affair so that she gets none of the blame from the families. You know how it is when marriages come to an end—there is almost always a pointing of fingers."

With this prediction delivered, Mma Potokwane reached for her teacup and took a long draught of tea. "Do you think I might be right, Mma?"

Mma Ramotswe took a few moments to regain her composure. This was quite extraordinary. At last she said, "You are *very* right, Mma. You are . . . you are as right as it is possible to be. It is quite amazing."

Mma Potokwane took the compliment in her stride. "I thought so," she said. And then added, "Poor man. People are sometimes hard on men, you know. People forget that sometimes men are innocent."

Mma Ramotswe agreed. "It is very important not to judge people by what they appear to be," she said. "There are many nice men around, Mma. Many."

"That is certainly true," said Mma Potokwane. "Mr. J.L.B. Matekoni, for one. My own husband. He may have one or two faults, but we are all human, Mma Ramotswe."

"We are definitely all human," said Mma Ramotswe. And she added, for the avoidance of all doubt, "That is well known, I think."

She was astonished by Mma Potokwane's deductive power. She had always admired her friend's ability to understand situations and to work out what was happening, but this went far beyond anything she had witnessed before. While Mma Ramotswe reflected on this, Mma Potokwane poured more tea, and cut her friend another slice of fruit cake. This helping was not quite as large as the initial one, but was generous enough—about thirty-five degrees this time. As Mma Ramotswe took her first bite, it occurred to her to ask about Mma Potokwane's pumpkins. On their walk, they had not reached the patch where these grew, but she was keen to find out how they were doing. Pumpkins, like everything else, liked rain, and would be benefitting greatly from the recent downpours. When was the agricultural show? Would they soon be sweeping the board at that?

She knew immediately that something was wrong. Mma Potokwane frowned, and then shook her head. "The show was two days ago," she said.

Mma Ramotswe waited.

"There were some other pumpkins," Mma Potokwane went on. "They were much bigger than mine. I had five, and I entered the biggest one. But there was another pumpkin that was bigger."

Mma Ramotswe sympathised. "I am sorry, Mma. I was hoping that you would win. Your pumpkins looked very impressive when I saw them that time. But . . ." What was there to say? Some pumpkins were bigger than others—it was the way of the world that this should be so. One could never tell with these things, and it was best not to hope for too much.

"You know who won?" asked Mma Potokwane.

Mma Ramotswe was silent. There was something ominous in the tone of Mma Potokwane's voice.

No, it was impossible. Surely not. No.

THERE WAS ONE MORE important thing for Mma Ramotswe to do that day, and that was to pay a visit to Mma Modise. She had not been looking forward to this encounter, but took the view, quite correctly, that it was not something that could be put off. There was always a temptation to avoid difficult meetings with clients, but experience had taught her that the more you delayed these matters, the more complicated they became. So, after she had left Mma Potokwane's office, she drove straight to the Modise house, having first ascertained that Mma Modise would be in.

"So you are back from visiting your sister," Mma Ramotswe said as Mma Modise showed her into her living room. "I hope that your visit went well, Mma."

Mma Modise made a dismissive gesture. "That sister of mine talks and talks, Mma. She never stops. I feel like putting beeswax in my ears so that I cannot hear her."

Mma Ramotswe could not help frowning. How could anybody talk about her sister—her own flesh and blood—in such an uncharitable way? If you have a sister—or a brother, indeed—you should be grateful. And if that sister or brother should talk too much, then you should remind yourself how fortunate you are that they have the breath to do all that talking. We all have a long time of silence ahead of us in the grave—before then, we should be happy to listen to what our brothers and sisters have to say.

"Well, you are back now," said Mma Ramotswe. "And I thought I should report to you on that matter you consulted me about."

Mma Modise smiled. "You are speaking very formally, Mma," she said. "I take it that you mean about my badly behaving husband."

Mma Ramotswe bit her lip. "I am not sure that I would describe your husband in those terms, Mma."

Mma Modise's lip curled. "Well, I would, Mma Ramotswe. I take it that you came round here while I was away."

Mma Ramotswe nodded. "I did, Mma. But before we discuss that, may I ask you if you have been in touch with Maria?"

"I have only just come back," began Mma Modise. And then she stopped herself. She had not been thinking. How could Mma Ramotswe know about Maria?

She struggled to recover her composure. "Who is this Maria, Mma Ramotswe? I do not know any Marias."

"Well," said Mma Ramotswe, "she knows you."

The two women stared at one another. Neither seemed ready to look away. But then Mma Modise's gaze slipped away.

Mma Ramotswe pressed her advantage. "I came to the house, Mma," she said. "I found your husband with the woman you had engaged to trap him. But do you know what I found, Mma? I found that your husband, being a good man, was holding back. He could not get involved with that woman, whatever her wiles, because . . ." She paused, and then continued, "Because, Mma, he still loves you. He could not do anything that would hurt you. That is what I discovered."

Mma Modise's eyes were fixed firmly on the floor. She did not say anything.

"It is possible, Mma," Mma Ramotswe went on, "that you might consider your position. I cannot get under your skin, Mma. I cannot work out what you really think about your marriage. I think that your marriage has big problems, and it may be that there will be nothing that can be done about it. But it is also possible that the two of you may be able to do something about it. That is for you to think about, Mma. But there is one thing I would say to you, and that thing is this: if there is a man who loves you, then you should think very carefully before you give up on that man. That is all, Mma. That is the advice I am giving you from the No. 1 Ladies' Detective Agency. Think about it, Mma. If you are having an affair with somebody, think about whether it is worth it. If you have lost your love for your husband, think about whether any of that love can be recovered. We cannot do any of that for you, Mma. We are a detective agency—we are not menders of souls. All we can say is that it is best not to be unkind in this life. That is all, Mma."

THAT EVENING, Mma Ramotswe and Mr. J.L.B. Matekoni sat on their verandah and watched the sky turn from blue to pink and finally to the colour of darkness, to the colour of night. There were evenings, perhaps the majority of them, when there was not much to talk about—or not much of any consequence. On such evenings, they were content to sit and think together and not give voice to their thoughts. It was perfectly possible, Mma Ramotswe felt, for those who were happily married—as they undoubtedly were—to think together, not to say anything, and then to discover that they had been thinking about the same things, and had, as it happened, agreed. On this evening, though, there was something that needed to be discussed.

"Your friend, Mogorosi," she said, trying hard to sound casual.

She saw him become tense. You could always tell when your words were worrying people. They stiffened. It was unmistakeable.

"Mogorosi?"

"Yes. How is he doing? Have the doctors finished with him?"

Mr. J.L.B. Matekoni nodded. "He was lucky, I think."

"Very," said Mma Ramotswe. "Of course, he was very unlucky to be bitten in the first place. When you're dealing with that sort of snake—"

He interrupted her. "He spoke to me, Mma. He has said he is very sorry. He told me that he had spoken to you about it."

She held her breath. She had not been looking forward to this conversation. She knew that they would have to have it, but she had been dreading it. Now, it seemed, Mogorosi had done all the hard work.

"He has said that he is sorry?"

"Oh, yes. He said that."

"Good."

She heard him breathing. She could tell that he was still upset.

"And you have forgiven him, Mr. J.L.B. Matekoni?"

They heard a bird in the tree immediately outside the verandah.

"That bird is making a fuss about something," said Mr. J.L.B. Matekoni. And then he said, "Yes, I have forgiven him. And I have resigned from that board. I am far too busy to do that sort of thing. There are all those cars to fix . . ."

"You are quite right, Rra. There are many cars to fix."

Mma Ramotswe reached out to touch her husband. She put her hand on his. He held it. It would not be necessary to say anything more about that, she decided. Forgiveness spoke more eloquently than any words. And forgiveness and the holding of hands—just like this—went well together.

She turned to something different. "Mma Potokwane gave me

one of her pumpkins. I have cooked it for tonight. I have cooked it for you."

He smiled. "She told me about them. She was very proud of them. Wasn't she entering them in that agricultural show they have out there?"

"She was."

Silence. Then, he said, "She didn't win, did she?"

Mma Ramotswe shook her head. "Pumpkins are for eating, though—they are not just for show."

"That is absolutely right, Mma Ramotswe. That is . . ."

"Well known," supplied Mma Ramotswe. She hesitated. It had to be said, and she said it now, quickly, so as to get it over with. "Violet Sephotho won. The best pumpkin in the show. She won the prize."

Mr. J.L.B. Matekoni made a strange noise. It was not a noise that Mma Ramotswe had heard before. It was a sort of choking noise.

"Are you all right?" she asked.

He nodded. "I was just clearing my throat."

Then Mma Ramotswe laughed. "You know something, Mr. J.L.B. Matekoni? I am happy for Violet Sephotho."

He gave her a sideways look, but the look became a smile—the smile of a man who knows what we need to do, and is prepared to do it. "So am I," he said.

They sat there for several more minutes. Then they got up and went inside, into the kitchen, where, on top of the stove, in a large cooking pot, their evening meal awaited them.

afrika
afrika afrika
afrika afrika afrika
afrika afrika
afrika

ABOUT THE AUTHOR

Alexander McCall Smith is the author of the No. 1 Ladies' Detective Agency novels and a number of other series and stand-alone books. His works have been translated into more than forty languages and have been bestsellers throughout the world. He lives in Scotland.